UNREAL!
Eight Surprising Stories

Paul Jennings

PUFFIN BOOKS

To Claire

PUFFIN BOOKS
Published by the Penguin Group
Penguin Books USA Inc., 375 Hudson Street, New York, New York 10014, U.S.A.
Penguin Books Ltd, 27 Wrights Lane, London W8 5TZ, England
Penguin Books Australia Ltd, Ringwood, Victoria, Australia
Penguin Books Canada Ltd, 10 Alcorn Avenue, Toronto, Ontario, Canada M4V 3B2
Penguin Books (N.Z.) Ltd, 182–190 Wairau Road, Auckland 10, New Zealand

Penguin Books Ltd, Registered Offices: Harmondsworth, Middlesex, England

First published in Australia by Penguin Books Australia Ltd., 1985
First published in the United States of America by Viking Penguin,
a division of Penguin Books USA Inc., 1991
Published in Puffin Books, 1993

1 3 5 7 9 10 8 6 4 2

LIBRARY OF CONGRESS CATALOGING-IN-PUBLICATION DATA

Jennings, Paul, 1943–
Unreal!: eight surprising stories / Paul Jennings. p. cm.
"First published by Penguin Books Australia, 1985"—Verso t. p.
Contents: Without a shirt—The strap box flyer—Skeleton on the
dunny—Lucky lips—Cow dung custard—Lighthouse blues—Smart
ice cream—Wunderpants.
ISBN 0-14-034910-3
1. Children's stories, Australian. 2. Fantastic fiction, Australian.
[1. Supernatural—Fiction. 2. Short stories.]
I. Title.
[PZ7.J429872Uo 1993]
[Fic]—dc20 92-44713 CIP AC

Printed in the United States of America

CONTENTS

WITHOUT A SHIRT

Mr Bush looked at the class. 'Brian Bell,' he said. 'You can be the first one to give your History talk.'

My heart sank. I felt sick inside. I didn't want to do it; I hated talking in front of the class. 'Yes, Mr Bush without a shirt,' I said. Sue Featherstone (daughter of the mayor) giggled. Slowly I walked out to the front of the class. I felt like death warmed up. My mouth was dry. 'I am going to talk about my great great grandfather.' I said. 'He was a sailor. He brought supplies to Warrnambool in his boat without a shirt.'

Thirty pairs of eyes were looking at me. Sue Featherstone was grinning. 'Why didn't he wear a shirt?' she asked. She knew the answer. She knew all right. She just wanted to hear me say it.

'His name was Byron. People called him Old Ben Byron without a shirt.'

'Why did they call him Old Ben Byron without a shirt?' Sue asked with a smirk. 'That's a funny name.'

'Don't tease him,' said Mr Bush. 'He is doing his best.'

She was a mean girl, that Sue Featherstone. Real mean. She knew I couldn't help saying 'without a shirt'. After I had finished saying something I always said 'without a shirt'. All my life I had done it – I just couldn't help it. Don't ask me why. I don't know why; I just couldn't stop myself. I had been to dozens of doctors. None of them knew what caused it and none of them could cure me. I hated doing it. Everyone laughed. They thought I was a bit queer.

I looked at Sue Featherstone. 'Don't be mean,' I said. 'Stop stirring. You know I can't stop saying "without a shirt" without a shirt.'

The whole grade cracked up. A lot of the kids tried not to laugh, but they just couldn't stop. They thought it was very funny. I went red in the face. I wished I was dead – and I wished that Sue Featherstone was dead too. She was the worst one in the form. She was always picking on me.

'Okay, Brian,' said Mr Bush. 'You can do your talk on Wednesday. You might be feeling a bit better by then.' I went and sat down. Mr Bush felt sorry for me. They all felt sorry for me. Everyone except Sue Featherstone, that is. She never thought about anyone except herself.

2

I walked home from school with Shovel. Shovel is my dog. He is called Shovel because he loves to dig holes. Nothing can stop him digging holes. He digs up old rubbish and brings it home and leaves it on the doorstep.

Once the man next door went fishing. He had a sack of mussels which he used for bait. When he got home he left them in the boot of his car and forgot about them. Two weeks later he found them – or I should say they found him. What a stink. Boy, were they on the nose! He had to bury them in his back yard. The next day Shovel dug them up and brought them home for me. He was always giving me presents like that. I didn't have the heart to punish him; he meant well. I just patted him on the head and said, 'Good boy without a shirt.'

Shovel was a great dog – terrific in fact. I am the first to admit that he didn't look much. He only had one eye, and half of one ear was gone. And he was always scratching. That wasn't his fault. It was the fleas. I just couldn't get rid of the fleas. I bought flea collars but they didn't work. I think that was because Shovel loved to roll in cow manure so much.

Apart from those few little things you wouldn't find a better dog than Shovel. He was always friendly and loved to jump up on you and give you a lick on the face. Mum and I would never give him up. He was all that we had left to remember Dad by. Shovel used to belong to Dad once. But Dad was killed in a car accident. So now there was just me, Shovel and Mum.

When I reached home I locked Shovel in the back yard. It didn't look much like a back yard, more like a battle field with bomb holes all over it. Shovel had dug holes everywhere. It was no good filling them in; he would just dig them out again. I went into the kitchen to get a drink. I could hear Mum talking to someone in the lounge. It was Mrs Featherstone (wife of the mayor). She owned our house. We rented it from her. She was tall and skinny and had blue hair. She always wore a long string of pearls (real) and spoke in a posh voice.

'Mrs Bell,' she was saying. 'I'm afraid you will have to find another place to live. It just won't do. That dog has dug holes everywhere. The back yard looks like the surface of the moon. Either you get rid of the dog or you leave this house.'

'We couldn't do that,' said Mum. 'Brian loves that dog. And it used to belong to his father. No, we couldn't give Shovel away.'

Just then Shovel appeared at the window. He had something in his mouth. 'There is the dreadful creature now,' said Mrs Featherstone. 'And what's that in its mouth?'

I rushed into the room. 'Don't worry,' I said. 'It's only Tibbles without a shirt.'

'Tibbles?' squeaked Mrs Featherstone. 'What is Tibbles?'

'Our cat,' I told her. 'It died six months ago and I buried it at the bottom of the yard without a shirt.'

Mrs Featherstone screamed and then she fainted. I don't know what all the fuss was about. It was only a dead cat. I know that Tibbles didn't look quite the same as when she was alive, but was that any reason to go and faint?

Anyhow, that is how we got kicked out of our house. And that is why we had to go and live in the cemetery.

3

When I say that we had to live in a cemetery I don't mean that we lived in a grave or anything like that. No, we lived in a house in the middle of the cemetery. It was a big, dark old house. Once the caretaker lived there, but he was gone now and no one else wanted to live in it. That's why the rent was cheap. It was all that we could afford. Mum was on the pension and we didn't have much money.

'You'll be happy here,' said the estate agent to Mum. 'It's very quiet. And it's the cheapest house in town.'

'I don't think that anyone can be happy in a grave-yard,' said Mum. 'But it will have to do for now. It's all we can afford.'

The agent walked off to his car. He was smiling about something. Then he looked at Shovel. 'I hope your dog doesn't dig holes,' he said. 'It's not a good idea for dogs that live in cemeteries to dig holes.' He thought he had said something really funny. He was still laughing as he drove out of the gate.

'Big joke without a shirt,' I called out after him.

The next day we moved in. I had a little room at the top of the house. I looked out over the graves. I could see the sea close by. The cemetery was next to the beach – we just had to walk over the sand dunes and there we were at Lady Bay Beach.

I went up to my room and started to work on my talk for school. I decided to write the whole thing out. That way I could make sure that I didn't have any 'without a shirts' in it. I didn't want to give Sue Featherstone the chance to laugh at me again. The only trouble was that the last time I tried this it didn't work. I still said the 'without a shirts' anyway. Still, it was worth a try – it might work this time. This is what I wrote.

OLD BEN BYRON

Old Ben Byron was my great great grandfather. He was the captain of a sailing ship. He sailed in with all sorts of goods for the town. He was one of the early settlers. This town is only here because of men like Ben Byron.

One day a man fell overboard. My great great grandfather jumped over to help him. The man was saved. But Old Ben Byron was swept away. He drowned. His body was never found.

I know this might seem a bit short for a talk at school. It is. But something happened that stopped me writing any more.

Shovel had been gone for some time; I was starting to worry about him. I hoped he wasn't scratching around near any of the graves. I looked out the window and saw him coming. I ran downstairs and let him in. He ran straight up to my room and dropped something on the floor. It was a bone.

4

I picked up the bone and looked at it. It was very small and pointed – just one little white bone. I could tell it was old. I knew I had seen a bone like that somewhere before, but I just couldn't think where. A funny feeling started to come over me. I felt lonely and lost, all alone. I felt as if I was dead and under the sea, rolling over and over.

My hand started to shake and I dropped the bone. I stared down at the bone on the floor. I was in bare feet and the bone had fallen right next to my little toe. Then I knew what sort of bone it was – it was a bone from some-one's toe. It was a human toe bone.

'Oh no,' I said to Shovel. 'What have you done? Where have you been digging? You bad dog. You have dug up a grave. Now we are in trouble. Big trouble. If anyone finds out we will be thrown out of this house. We will have nowhere to live without a shirt.'

I put on my shoes and ran outside. The strange feeling left me as soon as I closed the bedroom door. I only felt sad when I was near the bone. Outside it was cold and windy. I could hear the high seas crashing on the other side of the sand dunes. 'Show me where you got it,' I yelled at Shovel. 'Show me which grave it was without a shirt.' Shovel didn't seem to listen; he ran off over the sand dunes to the beach and left me on my own. I looked at all the graves. There were thousands and thousands of them. It was a very old cemetery and most of the graves were overgrown.

I started walking from one grave to the other trying to find signs of digging. I searched all afternoon. But I found nothing. I couldn't find the place where Shovel had dug up the bone.

In the end I walked sadly back to the house. I didn't know what to do with the bone. If anyone found it there would be a terrible fuss. We would be forced to leave the cemetery and would have nowhere to live.

When I reached the house Shovel was waiting for me. He was wagging his tail. He looked pleased with himself. He was covered in sand, and in his mouth he had another tiny bone. 'The beach,' I shouted. 'You found it at the beach without a shirt.' I snatched the bone from Shovel. As soon as I touched the bone the same sad feeling came over me. I felt lost and alone. I wanted something but I didn't know what it was.

It was another toe bone. I carried it up to my room and put it next to the other one. The feeling of sadness grew less. 'That's strange without a shirt,' I said to

Shovel. I picked up the second bone and put it outside the door. The feeling came back. It was very strong. I opened the door and put the two bones together again. I didn't feel quite so sad. 'These bones are not happy unless they are together,' I said. 'They want to be together without a shirt.'

5

I decided to have a serious talk to Shovel. I took his head between my hands. 'Listen,' I said. 'You have to show me where you found these bones. I will have to fill in the hole. You can't go digging up dead bodies all over the place. You just can't without a shirt.' Shovel looked at me with that big brown eye. I had the feeling that Shovel knew more about this than I did. He ran over to the door and started scratching at it. 'Okay,' I told him. 'I'll come with you. But first I will hide these bones without a shirt.' I put the two toe bones in a drawer with my socks. They still felt sad. So did I. As soon as I closed the drawer the feeling went.

We headed off to the beach. It was blowing a gale. The sand blew into my eyes and ears. I didn't know what to expect – maybe a big hole that Shovel had dug, with a skeleton in the bottom. Maybe a body washed up on the beach.

We climbed over the sand dunes and down to the shore. There was no one else on the beach. It was too cold. 'Well,' I said to Shovel, 'show me where you got the bones without a shirt.' He ran off into the sand dunes to a small hole. It was only as deep as my hand. There was no grave, just this small hole. I dug around with my hand but there were no other bones. 'That's good,' I told Shovel. 'There is no grave, and there is no body. Just two toe bones. Tomorrow I will bury them and that will be the end of it without a shirt.'

Shovel didn't listen. He ran off to the other end of the beach. It was a long way but I decided to follow him. When I reached him he was digging another hole. He found two more toe bones. I picked them up and straight away the sad, sad feeling came over me. 'They want to be with the others,' I said. 'See if you can find any more without a shirt.'

Shovel ran from one end of the beach to the other. He dug about thirty holes. In each hole he found one or two bones; some of them were quite big. I found an old plastic bag on the beach and put the bones in it. By the time it was dark the bag was full of unhappy bones. I felt like crying and I didn't know why. Even Shovel was sad. His tail was drooping. There wasn't one wag left in it.

I started to walk up the sand dunes towards home. Shovel didn't want to go; he started digging one more hole. It was a deep hole. He disappeared right inside it. At last he came out with something in his mouth, but it wasn't a bone. It was a shoe – a very old shoe. It wasn't anything like the shoes that you buy in the shops. It had a gold buckle on the top. I couldn't see it properly in the dark. I wanted to take it home and have a good look at it.

'Come on, Shovel,' I said. 'Let's go home. Mum will be wondering where we are without a shirt.' I picked up the bag and we walked slowly back to the house.

6

I put the two toe bones in the bag with the rest of them. Then I put the bag in my cupboard and shut the door. I felt much happier when the bones were locked away.

They were unhappy and they made me unhappy. I knew what the trouble was: they wanted to be with all the other bones. I guessed that they were all buried in different places along the beach.

I looked at the shoe; it was all twisted and old. It had been buried in the sand dunes for a long time. I wondered whose it was. Then I noticed something – two initials were carved into the bottom. I could just read them. They were 'B.B.'

'Ben Byron,' I shouted. 'The bones belong to my great great grandfather without a shirt.'

I suddenly thought of something – Ben Byron's shoe had reminded me. Tomorrow was Wednesday; I had to give my history talk at school. I groaned. I knew that I wouldn't be able to sleep worrying about it. And the more I worried the more nervous I would get. The more nervous I got the worse I would feel. The last time I gave a talk at school I got one out of ten. One out of ten. You couldn't get much lower than that.

Then I had an idea – I would take along the shoe. I would tell everyone I had found Ben Byron's shoe. That would make it interesting. I might even get three out of ten for my talk if I had the shoe. I put the shoe in my sock drawer and took the bag of bones out of the cupboard. I wanted to have a closer look at them.

I tipped the bones out into a pile on the floor. There were three long bones and a lot of small ones. The sad, lonely feeling came over me once more. I sat down on the bed and looked at the pile of sad bones. Then something happened that gave me a shock. The hair stood up on the back of my neck. I couldn't believe what I was seeing – the bones were moving. They were slowly moving around the floor. The bones were creeping around each other like a pile of snakes.

The bones sorted themselves out. They all fitted together. They formed themselves into a foot and a leg. All the bones were in the right order. I had the skeleton of Ben Byron's leg.

The leg didn't move. It just lay there on the floor. I sat on the bed looking at it for a long time. I can tell you I was scared – very scared. But I couldn't just leave the leg there; Mum might come in and see it. Anyway it was creepy having the skeleton of someone's leg lying on your bedroom floor. In the end I jumped up and swept all of the bones back into the bag and threw it into the corner of the room. Then I climbed into bed and put my head under the blanket. I tried to pretend that the bones weren't there.

7

The next day I had to give my talk at school. It went worse than I thought. It was terrible. I stood in front of the class for ages without saying anything; I was so scared that my knees were knocking. The words just wouldn't come out. 'What's up,' said Sue Featherstone. 'Haven't you got any shirts today?' A big laugh went up.

I managed to read the whole thing through to the end. I tried not to say anything else. I could feel it building up inside me – it was like a bomb waiting to go off. I kept my mouth closed tight but the words were trying to get out. My cheeks blew out and my face went red. 'Look at him,' laughed Sue Featherstone. 'He's trying not to say it.'

It was no good. The words exploded out. 'Without a shirt.'

I was embarrassed. I didn't know what to do. I grabbed the shoe. 'This is Ben Byron's shoe,' I said. 'It was washed ashore without a shirt.'

'It is not,' said Sue Featherstone . 'It's an old shoe that you found at the dump.'

Everything was going wrong. I would probably get nought out of ten for this talk. Then something happened that changed everything. A feeling of sadness swept over me. Everyone in the room felt it – they all felt sad. Then someone screamed. It was the leg – it was standing there at the door. It hopped across the room. My hands were shaking so much that I dropped the shoe. The leg hopped across the platform and into the shoe. It wanted the shoe.

Sue Featherstone looked at the skeleton leg and started shouting out. 'Get rid of it. Get rid of the horrible thing.'

The leg started hopping towards her. It hopped right up onto her desk. She screamed and screamed. Then she ran for the door. Everyone else had the same idea – they all ran for the door at the same time. There was a lot of yelling and pushing. They were all trying to get out of the door at once. They were scared out of their wits.

The leg bones chased the whole class across the playground and down the street. I have never heard so much yelling and screaming in all my life.

I was left alone in the classroom with Mr Bush. He just sat there shaking his head. After a while he said, 'I don't know how you did it, Brian. But it was a good trick. I give you ten out of ten for that talk. Ten out of ten.'

'Thanks, Mr Bush without a shirt,' I said.

8

When I got home from school the leg was waiting for me. It was just standing there in the corner of my room; it didn't move at all. But it was so sad and it made me sad. I felt as if I were a skeleton myself. I felt as if my bones were being washed away by the waves, as if they were being scattered along a long, sandy beach. I knew that this is what had happened to Ben Byron. His bones had been washed up and scattered along Lady Bay Beach.

I looked at Shovel. 'We have to find the rest of the bones,' I said. 'This leg will never have peace until all the bones are together again. We have to find the rest of the bones and we have to find them now without a shirt.'

I took a spade and a sack and walked towards the beach. Shovel came with me and so did the leg. It hopped slowly behind us making a plopping sound as it came. It still had the shoe on. It was lucky that there was no one on the beach – they wouldn't have believed their eyes if they had seen a boy, a dog and a skeleton leg walking along the beach. I could hardly believe it myself.

I didn't know where to start looking. But the leg did. It hopped across the beach and stood still where it wanted us to dig. We spent all afternoon following the leg around and digging holes. In every hole we found some bones. I went as fast as I could; I wanted to get rid of the sad feeling. Tears were running down my face because I was so unhappy. Every time I found some more bones I put them in the sack. The bones were glad to be together; I could tell that. But they were still sad. They would not be happy until I found the last one.

After a long time I found the last bone. It was the skull. It was in a hole with an old shirt – a very old shirt. I had never seen one like it before. I put the skull and the shirt in the sack. Then I held open the top. The leg hopped into the sack with the other bones.

9

The feeling of sadness went as soon as the leg joined the other bones. The bones were happy, I was happy and so was Shovel.

'Now,' I said to Shovel. 'We have a job to do. We have to bury all the bones in the same hole without a shirt.'

I carried the bag of happy bones to a lonely place in the sand dunes, and Shovel and I started to dig a hole. We worked at it for hours and hours. At last it was deep enough. I took the bag of bones and tipped them into the grave. They fell into a pile at the bottom; then they started to move. They slithered around at the bottom of the hole. I should have felt scared but I didn't. I knew what was happening. The bones were joining up into a skeleton. After a while it was finished. The skeleton was whole. It lay still at the bottom of the grave looking up at me. It didn't look as if it was at peace. There was something else – it wanted something else. I looked in the sack. The shirt was still there.

I threw the shirt into the hole. 'Don't worry,' I said. 'I won't bury you without a shirt.'

The bones started to move for the last time. The skeleton moved onto its side with the shirt under its head. It was in a sleeping position. It was very happy. Music seemed to come up out of the grave – silent music. I could hear it inside my head.

We filled in the grave and smoothed down the sand. I decided to say a few words; after all, it was a sort of a funeral. I looked out to sea. I could feel tears in my eyes. This is what I said. 'Here lie the bones of Ben Byron. At peace at last. Beside this beautiful bay.'

Shovel looked up at me. He seemed to be smiling.

'Hey,' I yelled. 'I didn't mention a shirt. I didn't say it.'

And I never did again.

THE STRAP BOX FLYER

Hundreds of people were watching Giffen. They thought he was a bit mad. But they couldn't stop looking. He was very interesting.

Giffen went over to his truck and got out a tube of glue. On the tube it said GIFFEN'S GREAT GLUE. IT WILL STICK ANYTHING. Giffen held the glue over his head. 'This is the best glue in the world,' he said. 'It can mend anything that is broken. Who has something that is broken?'

A small boy came out the front. He held up a bow and arrow. 'My bow is broken,' he said. 'And no one can fix it.' Giffen took the bow out of the boy's hand. He put a bit of glue on the broken ends and joined them together. Then he put the arrow in the bow and shot it into the air. The people were surprised. They all clapped and cheered.

'That's nothing,' Giffen told them. 'You haven't seen anything yet.' He went over to the back of his truck where he had a big crane. It had a rope on the end of it. Giffen grabbed the rope. He put a dab of glue on the end of it. Then he put the rope onto the roof of the car. 'This glue can hold up a car,' he told the crowd. He stepped into his truck and started up the crane. The car was lifted up into the air. The only thing that held the rope onto the car was the glue.

The crowd thought this was great. No one had ever seen glue like this before. 'Now,' said Giffen, 'who wants to buy some of Giffen's Great Glue?'

The crowd rushed foward. Everyone wanted some glue. They couldn't get it quick enough. They thought it was terrific. 'Get it while it lasts,' shouted Giffen. 'Only ten dollars a tube.'

Giffen sold two hundred tubes of glue. He made two thousand dollars in one day. The customers took their glue and went home to try it out.

'You fools,' said Giffen to himself. 'You will soon find out that the glue stops working after four hours.'

2

Miss Tibbs had bought a tube of Giffen's Great Glue. She was a very old lady. She lived all on her own. Most of her friends were dead. There was no one to help her to fix things up when they got broken. So she was very glad to have the glue.

Miss Tibbs collected china. She had spent all of her life saving pieces of china. She had plates and cups and saucers from all over the world. She also had little china dolls and toy animals. She had so many pieces that she didn't know where to put them all. This is why she wanted the glue. She wanted to put up a new shelf.

As soon as she got home Miss Tibbs went and fetched a piece of wood from the shed in her back garden. Then she put some of Giffen's Great Glue along the edge of the wood and stuck it onto the wall. It worked well. The shelf was very strong.

'This is wonderful glue,' she said. 'It dries straight away.' Miss Tibbs started to put her china pieces on to the shelf. She decided to put her favourite piece out first. It was a small china horse. She had owned it for many years. It had been given to her by her father before he died. Miss Tibbs loved this horse. She put it in the best spot, right in the middle of the shelf.

After she had put all of the other pieces out Miss Tibbs sat down and had a rest. She was very tired. She fell asleep in her armchair in front of the fire.

Four hours later Miss Tibbs was woken up by a loud crash. The glue had stopped working. The shelf had fallen off the wall and all of the china pieces were smashed.

Miss Tibbs went down onto her hands and knees. She started to pick up all of the broken pieces. Then she remembered her horse. Her precious horse. She looked for it among the bits. She couldn't find it. Then she found something that made her cry. A leg and a tail and a tiny head. The horse was smashed to pieces.

Miss Tibbs cried and cried. She got her tube of Giffen's Great Glue and threw it in the fire. Then she decided that she would go and find Giffen. She would tell him that his glue was no good. She would ask him to pay for the broken china.

She hurried back to the place where Giffen had been. But he was gone. There was no sign of him. She knew that he would never come back.

3

Another person who bought the tube of Giffen's Great Glue was Scott Bridges. He had bought it to mend his canoe. It had broken in half.

Scott's father had told him the canoe could not be repaired. He said that its back was broken. He told Scott to take it to the dump. But now that Scott had a tube of Giffen's Great Glue he knew that he could fix it.

The canoe was down at the lake. Scott went down there on his own. He didn't tell his father where he was going. He pulled the two pieces of the canoe together, and put Giffen's Great Glue along the join.

'Great,' yelled Scott. 'It's as good as new. This glue is fantastic.' He pushed the canoe into the water and climbed in. It floated well. It didn't leak at all. Scott began to paddle out into the middle of the lake. He was very happy. And excited. He paddled off as fast as he could go.

Scott was not allowed to go out into the canoe without a life jacket. But on this day he had forgotten. All that he could think about was the canoe and Giffen's Great Glue.

It was a sunny day and the time passed quickly. Soon four hours had passed. Scott noticed that some water was starting to leak into the canoe. He decided to start paddling for home. But it was too late. The glue had come unstuck. The canoe broke in two and sank.

The water was icy cold. Scott was frightened. It was a long way to the shore. 'Help,' he screamed at the top of his voice. But no one heard him. He was the only person on the lake.

Scott started to swim to shore. After a little while he began to get tired. His legs hurt and he had a pain in his stomach. His head went under the water. He tried to get back to the top. But it was no use. His lungs filled with water and he sank to the bottom of the lake.

That night when Scott did not come home his father called the police. Divers searched the lake. They found Scott's body. And the broken canoe. In the bottom of the canoe was a tube of Giffen's Great Glue.

4

Giffen was driving away in his truck. Very fast. He knew that he only had four hours to get away. Then the people who had bought the glue would start looking for him. He knew that they would be mad. He did not want them to catch him.

He decided to drive to Horsham. That was a long way off. They would not know about Giffen's Great Glue in Horsham. He could find some more suckers, and make some more money.

Two days later he arrived in Horsham. He took his truck to the centre of town. Then he put up a sign. The sign said:

TWO HUNDRED DOLLARS PRIZE

FOR ANYONE WHO CAN UNSTICK

GIFFEN'S GREAT GLUE

Soon two men arrived. They were both riding tractors. One of the men got down from his tractor. He walked over to Giffen and gave him two pieces of rope. 'Join these up with your glue,' he said. 'Then we will pull it apart.'

Giffen smiled to himself. 'Okay,' he said. 'I'll do it.' He put a dob of glue on the end of the two pieces of rope. Then he joined them together. The glue stuck fast.

The men took the rope that had been joined. They tied one end to each of the tractors. Then they started the tractors up. There was a lot of smoke and noise. A crowd started to gather. Everyone thought that the glue would break. But it didn't. The wheels on the tractors sent up blue smoke. The engines roared. But still the glue held.

Then there was a lound bang. The engine of one of the tractors had stopped. The other tractor started to drag it along the road. Everyone cheered at the top of their voices.

'Now,' said Giffen, 'who will buy my great glue?'

The crowd pushed forward. Everyone wanted some. The people waved their money. They pushed and shoved. Giffen sold three hundred tubes.

At last everyone went home. Except one man. A short, bald man with a friendly smile. 'Excuse me,' he said to Giffen. 'But I wonder if you would like to buy something from me?'

'What are you selling?' said Giffen in gruff voice.

'A Strap Box Flyer. It is a small box that will make people fly.'

5

Giffen didn't believe that there was a box that could make someone fly. There was no such thing. This man was trying to fool him. Still, he was interested. It might be a new sort of trick that he could use himself, to make money from the suckers. He looked at his watch. He had to get out of this town before the glue started to come unstuck. He had four hours left. There was plenty of time to talk to the little man.

'Okay,' said Giffen to the little man. 'Show me your Strap Box Flyer'

'Not here, someone might see us. Come home with me and I will show you how it works.'

Giffen followed the little man home to his house. It was a small cottage. It was very untidy. The grass was long and some of the windows were broken. Inside there was junk everywhere. There were tools, nuts and bolts, machines and bits of wire all over the floor.

'My name is Mr Flint,' said the little man. 'But everyone calls me Flinty.'

'I'm in a hurry, Flinty,' said Giffen. 'So let me see you do some flying.'

'Very well, very well,' replied Flinty. He went over to a shelf and took down a small box. Then he lifted up the carpet and pulled out a short strap. It looked like a watch band made out of silver.

'I keep the strap in one place, and the box in another,' said Flinty. 'That's to stop anyone stealing my invention. I have to screw the box onto the strap. It won't work unless both pieces are screwed together.'

Flinty fiddled around with the box and the strap. It took a long time. About half an hour. Giffen was getting worried. He did not want to stay much longer. The crowd would be mad when they found out that the glue did not work for long. At last Flinty finished. He had screwed the box onto the strap. He put it onto his arm. It looked just like a wrist watch, only bigger.

'Now,' said Flinty. 'Watch this.' Slowly he rose up off the floor. He went up about ten centimetres.

Giffen could not believe it. His eyes nearly popped out of his head. 'How high can you go?' he asked Flinty.

'As high as I want to.' Flinty floated up to the ceiling. Then he flew around the room, just like a cloud.

Giffen knew that he had to get the Strap Box Flyer. It was worth a fortune. He could make a lot of money if he had it.

'Why are you showing this to me?' Giffen asked Flinty.

'Because you are a great inventor,' said Flinty. 'You have invented Giffen's Great Glue. I am an inventor too. I have invented the Strap Box Flyer. We could be partners. You could help me make the Strap Box Flyer. And I could help you to make the glue.'

Giffen did not say anything. He was thinking. He wanted the Strap Box Flyer. But he couldn't stay in Horsham. Once four hours was up his glue would stop working. The things that people had mended would start falling to bits. They would come looking for him. He could even end up in jail.

'Have you got another Strap Box Flyer?' Giffen asked.

'Yes,' said Flinty. 'I have one more. You can try it out if you want to. But first I will have to assemble it. I will have to screw the strap onto the box.'

'That will take half an hour,' said Giffen. 'I will go and get my truck. Then I will be back to try out the Strap Box Flyer myself.' Giffen went off. He had decided to steal the Strap Box Flyer. He wanted to have the truck nearby for a quick getaway.

Giffen could not believe his luck. Once he had the Strap Box Flyer he would find out how it worked. Then he would make more of them. He could sell them for thousands of dollars each. He would make a fortune. Everyone would want one.

He ran back to his truck. Then he drove to Flinty's

house as fast as he could. The Strap Box Flyer was ready. There would just be time for a quick tryout and then he would have to leave town.

Flinty put the Strap Box Flyer onto Giffen's arm. 'Now,' he said. 'All you have to do is to think of where you would like to fly to.'

Giffen thought that he would like to fly over to his truck. It worked. He went gently flying through the air and landed on the roof of his truck. Flinty floated over and joined him. 'Great,' said Giffen. 'Really great. How high can we go with these things?'

'As high as you like,' said Flinty. 'As high as you like.'

7

Giffen forgot about everything except the Strap Box Flyer. He forgot about the time. He forgot about Giffen's Great Glue and he forgot about getting out of town quickly.

'Let's go up to the clouds,' he said to Flinty. And so they flew together. High into the sky. When they looked down the people looked like tiny ants. It was wonderful to fly so high.

Time passed quickly. Hours went by. It started to get dark. Giffen decided that he would wait until it was night. Then he would be able to get away from Flinty. He would just fly off and lose Flinty in the dark. Then he would drive off in his truck and never come back. He could take the Strap Box Flyer to bits and find out how it worked. Then he could make a lot more of them. And sell them. Then he would be rich.

Flinty flew over to Giffen. 'We are very high,' he said.

'We can't go much higher than this. There will be no air to breathe.'

Giffen looked down. They were so high that he could not see the ground. They were above the clouds.

'I have only made two Strap Box Flyers so far,' said Flinty, 'and yours is the best of the two.'

'Why is that?' asked Giffen.

'Because I joined it together with Giffen's Great Glue.'

Giffen was just in time to see his Strap Box Flyer break into bits. Then he started to fall.

He screamed all the way down.

SKELETON ON THE DUNNY

All right. So you want to hear the story of the ghost on the dunny. Everybody wants to know about it, so I am going to tell it for the last time. I will put it on this tape recording.

Someone else can write it down. My spelling is not too good. And anyway, I haven't got the time for a lot of writing.

I am giving you a warning: this is not a polite story. If your feelings get hurt it will be your own fault. I call a spade a spade. And I call a dunny a dunny.

If you live in Australia, you know what a dunny is. It is a toilet. A lavatory. Other names for it are throne, loo, WC, jerry, and thunder box. I have heard it called other things, but I won't mention them here. I am not a rude person; I just get to the point.

Some dunnies are outside. An outside dunny is usually at the bottom of the garden, a long way from the house. If it rains you get wet. If it is night time you have to get a torch and go there in the dark. When you have finished you have to pull a chain to make it flush. There are no buttons or anything flash like that.

2

Anyway, I must get back to the story. It all started when I was fourteen years old. My parents died in a car accident and I went to live with my Aunty Flo. She lived in the country, at Timboon.

I was pretty broken up – miserable, in fact. One minute I was as happy as Larry, with a mother and a father, living in a big house in the city. The next minute I was with Aunty Flo in the bush.

Aunty Flo was nice. It wasn't her fault; I just felt low because of what happened. That sort of thing is very hard to take.

My new home was very old. It was a big wooden house with a verandah all around it. It had a tin roof; you could hear the rain falling on it at night.

Inside the house it was very dark. Gloomy. Every doorway had wooden beads hanging down on strings. There were old photos all over the walls, pictures of glum men staring down at you. In the hall was a tall clock, a grandfather clock. It ticked loudly. The house was so quiet that you could hear the ticking in every room. For some reason you always felt like whispering. It was like a library.

School had finished; it was the holidays. There wasn't much to do. I didn't know anybody in the town, so most days I went hunting rabbits. Or snakes.

Aunty Flo was very good to me. She liked me. 'Bob,' she would say, 'you need fattening up.' She made jam tarts and little cakes with icing, and set them up on the table with neat napkins. She was a very good cook, and very old. She didn't know much about boys. She let me go wherever I liked. She only had one rule. 'Be home for tea on time.'

I liked Aunty Flo. But I didn't like her outside dunny.

3

One day Aunty Flo took me aside. She was waving a bit of paper and she looked very serious. 'It is very sad about your parents, Bob,' she said. 'I am worried about your future. If I die there will be no one to look after you.'

She was a good hearted old girl. A tear ran down her face. 'Anyway,' she said, 'I have made some plans. This is my will. It tells what will happen to my things if I die. I have left everything to you. If I die you will get the lot: the house and my money.'

I didn't know what to say. I looked at my shoes. She kept talking with tears in her eyes. 'The only thing you won't get is a painting I used to have. You can't have it because it is gone. Stolen. It was in my family for a long time. It was worth a lot of money – very valuable. It was a painting of this house. I wanted you to have it.'

I pretended not to notice her tears. 'Who stole it, Aunty?' I asked.

'I don't know,' she answered. 'I went away to England for two years. A man called Old Ned lived in the house and looked after everything for me. But when I came back he was dead, and the painting was gone.'

I asked Aunty Flo how Ned died. 'I don't know,' she said. 'I found him on the toilet at the bottom of the garden. He had been there for a year. There wasn't much left of him – just a skeleton, sitting on the toilet.'

28

4

Well, that was nice. That was very nice. Now I had to go and sit in an outside dunny where someone had died.

I didn't like going to that loo at the best of times. You had to walk down a long path, overgrown with weeds. Trees stuck out and scratched your face. When you got inside it was very dark – there was no light globe. There were cobwebs. And no toilet paper, just a nail on the wall with newspaper hanging on it. It wasn't even worth reading the paper. It was only the *Age*. Very boring.

Those cobwebs had me worried too. There could be spiders – redback spiders. Redbacks are poisonous. I knew that song about redbacks on the toilet seat. It wasn't funny when your pants were down, I can tell you that.

Redbacks, cobwebs, stories about skeletons and no one around. I didn't like sitting there with the door closed, especially at night. At night it was creepy.

One day I was in the dunny paying a visit. There wasn't much to do. I started counting holes in the wall. A lot of knots had fallen out of the wood. They were little round holes that let in a bit of light. I had counted up to hole number twenty when I saw something that made my hair stand on end.

An eye was looking at me. Staring at me through the hole.

It was not just any old eye. I could see right through it. I could see the trees on the other side of it. It was not a human eye.

I pulled up my pants fast. No one has ever pulled up their pants that fast before. I ran up the path and back to the house like greased lightning.

I told Aunty Flo about it, but she didn't believe me. 'Rubbish,' she said. 'There is nothing down there. It's just your imagination.'

5

You can imagine how I felt. Very nice. Very nice indeed, I don't think. I was not going down there again. No way. Just think how you would feel at the bottom of the garden, in the dark, sitting on a dunny where someone had died. Not only died, but turned into a skeleton. Then there were cobwebs, redback spiders and eyes. Eyes looking at you through holes in the walls.

I made up my mind. I wasn't going down there again. Ever.

I didn't go there for a week. Then I started feeling a bit crook. I felt terrible. 'You're not looking well,' said Aunty Flo. 'You've not been regular, have you, dear? You'd better have some medicine.'

The medicine fixed me up all right. I got the runs. I spent most of the day sitting down there. But what I was really worried about were the nights.

Sure enough it happened: I had to go to the loo in the night. I took a torch and went slowly down the dark path. The trees were rustling and something seemed to be moaning. I told myself that it was a bird. I hoped that it was a bird. It had to be a bird.

At last I reached the dunny. I went inside, shut the door, and locked it. I had no sooner sat down than something terrible happened. The torch slowly went out. The batteries were flat – as flat as a tack.

I think I should tell you what happens to me when I get scared. My teeth start to chatter. They go clickety click. Very loudly.

So there I was, sitting in the dark with my teeth chattering. I tried to stop it, but I couldn't. You must have been able to hear the noise a mile away.

I started to think about creepy things. Eyes. Bats. Vampires. Murderers. I was scared to death. I wanted to get out of there. My teeth were chattering louder and louder.

Then the moon came out. Moonbeams shone through the space on top of the door. I felt a bit better – but only for a second. I looked up and my heart froze. A face was looking at me. An old man's face. He had a beard and was wearing an old hat. He just stood there staring at me over the top of the door. And even worse, much worse, the moon was shining right through him. I could see through him. He didn't block out the moonlight at all.

6

I couldn't get out. The old man was on the other side of the door. I was trapped. I started screaming out, 'Aunty Flo, Aunty Flo. Help! Help! A ghost!'

The face looked startled. Then it disappeared. I didn't waste any time – I kicked open the door and ran out. But I fell flat on my face. I had forgotten to pull my pants up.

When I finally pulled up my pants the ghost had gone. I tore up the path screaming out for Aunty Flo.

Aunty Flo didn't believe me. She knew I was scared. But she didn't believe there was a ghost. 'Nonsense,' she said, 'there are no such things as ghosts. I have been going down there for sixty years, and I have never seen one.'

I tried to make the best of it. I smiled. A weak smile, but a smile. Aunty Flo did not smile back. She was staring at me. Her mouth was hanging open. 'Bob,' she shouted. 'Bob. One of your teeth is missing. One of your beautiful teeth.'

I put my hand up to my mouth. Sure enough a front tooth was gone – broken clean off. I knew what had happened. My teeth had chattered so hard that the tooth had broken. That ghost had done it now. I was starting to get mad with that ghost.

Aunty Flo was upset. 'You must have done it when you fell over,' she said. She put some new batteries in the torch. Then we went to look for the tooth. There was no sign of it. There was no sign of the ghost either.

The next day we went to the dentist. He had bad news for me. 'You'll have to have a plate,' he said. 'The tooth is gone and the piece that is left is split.'

'What's a plate?' I asked.

'Like false teeth,' he told me. 'But you will only have one tooth that is false. And you will have to look after it. They cost a lot of money, so don't lose it. Clean it every night and put it in water when you go to bed. And don't break it by biting string or hard objects.'

The plate cost two hundred dollars. Can you believe that? Two hundred dollars. Aunty Flo had to pay up. It was a lot of money. She made sure I looked after that tooth. I had to clean it every night and every morning. She checked on it when I was in bed. Every night she looked at the tooth in the glass of water. If the plate wasn't clean she made me do it again. She wouldn't let me take it out of my mouth in the day. She thought I might lose it.

That ghost had caused a lot of trouble. I had lost a tooth. And Aunty Flo had wasted two hundred dollars.

7

I didn't see the ghost again for about a month. I stayed away from the bottom of the garden at night time. I only went in the day. He didn't come in the day any more. All the same, I made my visits very short.

I did a lot of thinking about that ghost. Who was he? Why was he hanging around a dunny? I asked Aunty Flo about Old Ned who had died down there. 'Aunty Flo,' I said one day. 'You know that old man who lived here when you lost your painting? What did he look like?'

She looked sadly at the place where her lost painting used to hang. And then she said, 'He always wore an old hat. And he had a beard. A long grey beard.'

I knew at once that the ghost was Old Ned. I felt a bit sorry for him. Fancy having your skeleton sitting on a dunny for a year.

All the same, I wished he would go away. I didn't want to see him again. But of course I did.

One night I just had to go. You know what I mean. I got my torch out and I went out into the dark, down to the bottom of the garden. I was scared – really scared. My teeth began to chatter again. They were really clacking.

I was worried about my plate. With all the clacking it might break. I took it out and held it in my hand. There I sat, tooth in hand, and my real teeth chattering enough to wake the dead. I left the dunny door open. If Old Ned showed up I wanted to get away quickly. I didn't want to be trapped.

I did the job that I went for. Then I pulled up my pants. I reached up and pulled the chain. As I did so I could feel someone watching me. My hands started to shake.

Badly. The plate slipped out of my hand and into the dunny. In a flash it was gone, flushed down the loo.

When I turned around I saw Old Ned standing there. I could see right through him – through his hat, through his beard, through his hands and his face.

He looked very sad – very sad indeed. I didn't run. I didn't feel quite so frightened now that I could see him properly. He was trying to say something. His mouth was moving, but no sound came out. And he was pointing. Pointing to the roof of the dunny. I looked up, but there was nothing to see. Just a rusty old roof.

'What do you want?' I heard myself say. 'Why are you hanging around this loo all the time?'

He couldn't hear me. He just kept pointing at the roof of the dunny. Then he started to fade. He just started to fade away in front of my eyes. Then he was gone – vanished.

I walked slowly up the path. I wasn't scared any more; not of the ghost. He looked harmless. But I was scared of something else. I was scared of what Aunty Flo was going to say when she found that my plate had gone.

8

The next morning I jumped out of bed early. I wrote a note for Aunty Flo. It said:

> Aunty Flo
> Gone for a ride on my bike.
> I will be back for tea.
>
> Bob.

I set out to look for my tooth. I wanted to find it before Aunty Flo knew that it was gone.

I knew where the sewerage farm was. It was twenty miles away to the north. My tooth had gone north.

It was a long way. The road was very dusty and hot. The paddocks were brown. All the cows were sitting under trees in the shade. There was no shade for me, but I kept riding.

By lunch time I could tell that I was getting close to the sewerage farm. I could smell it. It was a bad smell – a terrible smell. As I rode closer the smell got worse.

At last I reached the farm. It had a high wire fence around it. Inside were a lot of brown ponds. In the middle of all the ponds was a hut. Inside the hut I could see a man. He was writing at a desk.

That man had the worst job in the world. He was sitting down working in the middle of a terrible stink – a shocking stink. But he didn't seem to mind. I held my nose with one hand and knocked on the open door.

'Come in,' he said. 'What can I do for you?'

He was a little bald man with glasses. He looked friendly. He didn't seem to care that I was holding my nose. 'Excuse me,' I said. 'Have you seen a plate? Has a plate come through the sewer?' It was hard to talk with my hand holding my nose. It sounded as if I had a cold.

'A plate?' he said. 'No. A plate could not fit through the pipes. It would be too big.'

'Not that sort of plate,' I told him. 'Not a dinner plate. A mouth plate. A plate with a tooth on it. A false tooth.'

'Ah,' he said, and smiled. 'Why didn't you say. False teeth. Yes, we have false teeth.'

He went over to the wall. There were a lot of baskets there. They all had labels. One said 'pens and pencils'.

Another said 'watches'. He brought over a basket and dumped it in front of me. It was full of false teeth.

They were all dirty. They were brown. The man gave me a pair of tongs. I started to sort through them slowly. I felt a bit sick. I felt like throwing up. At last I found a plate with only one tooth on it. My precious plate! It looked yucky. It was brown and slimy. And it stank. I thought of where it had been. And where I found it.

I didn't know if I could ever put it in my mouth again. I wrapped it up in my handkerchief and rode slowly home.

When I reached home I went up to the bathroom. I scrubbed that plate. I scrubbed it and scrubbed it. It got a lot cleaner but it was still the wrong colour. The tooth was not white enough. Next I boiled it in water, but it was still a bit grey. That was as clean as I could get it.

I put it on the table and looked at it. I looked at it for a long time. Then I picked it up and closed my eyes. I shoved it in my mouth very quickly.

9

Old Ned had a lot to answer for. He had caused a lot of trouble. But all the same I felt sorry for him. It couldn't be fun hanging around a toilet. I wondered why he was there, and why he looked so sad. I decided that I would go and see him to have a talk. I wasn't scared of him any more.

I waited until Aunty Flo had gone to bed. Then I took out my torch and set out for the dunny. It was very windy and wild. Clouds were blowing across the moon. The trees were all shaking. Leaves blew into my face. It seemed a long way to the bottom of the garden.

When I reached the dunny it was empty. There was no sign of Old Ned. It was cold out in the wind, so I went inside and sat down.

I waited for a long time. The wind started to get stronger. It blew the door shut with a bang. The moon went behind a cloud. It was very dark.

The dunny started to shake. The wind was screaming and howling. Then the walls started to lean over. The wind was blowing the dunny over with me in it. There was a loud crash and the whole thing collapsed. It fell right over on its side. Everything went black.

When I woke up the wind had stopped. My head hurt. But I was all right. No broken bones. Someone was bending over me. It was Old Ned.

He was just the same as before. I could see right through him. But he was smiling. He looked happy. He was pointing at the roof of the dunny. It was all smashed up. I went over and had a look.

Under a piece of tin was a picture frame. It was Aunty Flo's missing painting, the stolen painting.

I picked up the painting and put it under my arm. Aunty Flo would be glad to get it back. Very glad.

I started to say thanks to Ned. But something was happening. He started to float up into the air. He was going straight up. He looked happy. Happy to be leaving the earth.

He floated up towards the moon. He grew smaller and smaller. At last I couldn't see him any more. He was gone. I knew he wouldn't be coming back.

10

Aunty Flo was very pleased to get her painting back. She was so happy that she cried. She hung it on the wall in its old spot. She kept looking at it all the time.

I didn't tell her about Old Ned. She wouldn't believe it anyway. But I think I know what happened.

Old Ned stole the painting. He hid it in the dunny roof. When he died he was in Limbo. He was not in this world because he was dead. He could not go to the next world because he had done something bad.

So he had to hang around the outside loo, hoping that Aunty Flo would find her painting. Now that she had got it back he was free to go. When he floated off into the air he was going to a happier place. Wherever that is.

Aunty Flo put in a new toilet. An inside one. It was all shiny and clean. A push-button job. No cobwebs, spiders or ghosts.

Well, that is just about the end of the story. Except for one thing.

One day I was looking at Aunty Flo's lost painting. It was a painting of her house in the old days, when it had just been built. It had no trees around it. Out the back you could see the outside dunny with the door open.

I looked very closely at that dunny in the picture. Someone was in it! Sitting down. I went and got a magnifying glass and looked again.

It was Old Ned, with his hat and his long beard. He looked happy. He had a smile on his face, and one eye closed.

He was winking at me.

LUCKY LIPS

Marcus felt silly. He was embarrassed. But he knocked
on the door anyway. There was no answer from inside
the dark house. It was as silent as the grave. Then he
noticed a movement behind the curtain; someone was
watching him. He could see a dark eye peering through a
chink in the curtain. There was a rustling noise inside
that sounded like rats' feet on a bare floor.

The door slowly opened and Ma Scritchet's face
appeared. It was true what people said – she looked like a
witch. She had hair like straw and her nose was hooked
and long. She smiled showing pointed, yellow teeth.

'Come in,' she said. 'I have been waiting for you.'

Marcus was not going to let this old woman fool him.
'How could you be expecting me?' he answered. 'No one
knew I was coming here.' He felt better now. He could
see that it was all a trick. She was a faker. A phoney. Did
she really expect him to believe that she knew he was
coming?

'I knew you were coming,' she said. 'And I know *why*
you have come.'

This time Marcus knew she was lying. He had not told anyone about his problem. There was not one person in the world that knew about it, it was too embarrassing. The other kids would laugh if they knew.

He decided to go home. But first he would stir this old bag up a bit. 'Okay, Ma,' he said. 'Why have I come?'

She looked him straight in the eye. 'You are sixteen years old,' she told him. 'And you have never been kissed.'

Marcus could feel his face turning red. He was blushing. She knew – she knew all about it. She must be able to read minds. The stories that were told about her must be true. He felt silly and small, and he didn't know what to do.

Ma Scritchet started to laugh, a long cackling laugh. It made Marcus shiver. 'Come with me,' she said. She led him along a dark, narrow passage and up some wooden stairs. The house was filled with junk: broken TV sets and old bicycles, piles of books and empty bottles. The stair rails were covered in cobwebs. They went into a small room at the top of the house.

Inside the room was a couch and a chair. Nothing else. It was not what Marcus had expected. He thought there would be a crystal ball on a round table and lots of junk and equipment for telling fortunes. The room was almost bare.

2

Ma Scritchet held out her hand. 'This will cost you twenty dollars,' she said to Marcus.

'I pay after, not before,' said Marcus. 'This could be a trick.'

'You pay before, not after,' said Ma Scritchet. 'I only help those that believe in me.' Marcus looked into her eyes. They were cold and hard. He took out his wallet and gave her twenty dollars, and she tucked it inside her dress. Then she said, 'Lie down on the couch.'

Marcus lay on the couch and stared at the ceiling. A tiny spider was spinning a web in the corner. Marcus felt foolish lying there on a couch in this old woman's house. He wished he hadn't come; he wanted to go home. But there was something about Ma Scritchet that made him nervous. And now that he had paid his twenty dollars he was going to get his money's worth. 'Well,' he said. 'I suppose that you want me to tell you about my problem.'

'No,' said Ma Scritchet. 'I will tell you about it. You just stay there and listen.' Marcus did as she said.

'You have never kissed a girl,' said the old woman in a low voice. 'You have tried plenty of times. But they always turn you down. They think you are stuck up and selfish. They don't like the things you say about other people. Some girls go out with you once, but when you get home to their front door they always say, "Thank you" and go inside.'

Marcus listened in silence. Most of it was true. He knew he wasn't stuck up and selfish, but the rest of it was right. He tried everything he could think of. He would take a girl to the movies and buy her chocolates. He would even pay for her to get in. But then, right at the end when they were saying 'good night', he would close his eyes, pucker up his lips and lean forward, to find himself kissing the closed front door of the girl's house. It was maddening. It was enough to make him spit. And it

41

had happened dozens of times. Not one girl would give him a kiss.

3

'Well,' said Marcus to Ma Scritchet. 'Can you help me? That's what I gave you the twenty dollars for.'

She smiled but said nothing. It was not a nice smile. It was a smile that made Marcus feel foolish. She stood up without a word and left the room, and Marcus could hear her footsteps clipping down the stairs. A minute or so later he heard her coming back. She came into the room and held out a small tube. 'Take this,' she said. 'It's just what you need. This will do the trick.'

Marcus took it out of her hand and looked at it. It was a stick of lipstick in a small gold container. 'I'm not wearing lipstick,' Marcus told her. 'You must think I'm crazy.' He sat up and jumped off the couch. This had gone far enough. He wondered if he could get his money back.

'Sit down, boy,' said Ma Scritchet in a cold voice. 'And listen to me. You put that on your lips and you will get all the kisses you want. It has no colour. It's clear and no one will be able to see it. But it will do the trick. It will work on any female. Just put some of that on your lips and the nearest girl will want to kiss you.'

Marcus looked at the tube of lipstick. He didn't know whether to believe it or not. It might work. Old Ma Scritchet could read his mind; she knew what his problem was without being told. This lipstick could be just what he needed. 'Okay,' he said. 'I'll give it a try. But it had better work. If it doesn't, I will be back for my twenty dollars.'

'It will work,' hissed Ma Scritchet. 'It will work better than you think. Now it's time for you to go. The session is over.' She led Marcus down the narrow stairs and along the passage to the front door. He stepped out into the sunlight. It was bright and made him blink. As Ma Scritchet closed the door she told Marcus one more thing. 'This lipstick will only work once on each person. One girl: one kiss. That's the way it works.'

She closed the door in his face without saying another thing. Once more the old house was quiet.

4

Marcus kept the lipstick for a week before he used it. When he got home to his room with his record player and the posters on the wall, the whole thing seemed like a dream. The old house and Ma Scritchet were from another world. He wondered whether or not the visit had really happened, but he had the lipstick to prove that it had.

He held it in his hand. It had a strange appearance and he found that it glowed in the dark. He put it in a drawer and left it there.

Later that week a new girl started at Marcus's school. Her name was Jill. Marcus didn't waste any time; he asked her out for a date on her first day at school. She didn't seem too keen about going with him, but she was shy and didn't want to seem unfriendly, especially as she didn't know anyone at the school. In the end she agreed to go to a disco with him on Friday night.

Marcus arranged to meet Jill inside the disco. That way he wouldn't have to pay for her to get in. It wasn't a bad turn and Jill seemed to enjoy it. As he danced

Marcus could feel the lipstick in his pocket. He couldn't forget about it; it annoyed him. It was like having a stone in his shoe.

At eleven o'clock they decided to go home. It was only a short walk back to Jill's house. As they walked, Jill chatted happily; she was glad that she had made a new friend so quickly. Marcus started to feel a bit guilty. He fingered the lipstick in his pocket. Should he use it? He remembered something about stolen kisses. Was he stealing a kiss if he used the lipstick? Not really – if it worked Jill would be kissing him of her own free will. Anyway, it probably wouldn't work. Old Ma Scritchet had probably played a trick on him. He would never know unless he tried it. He just had to know if the lipstick worked, and this was his big chance.

As they went inside the front gate of Jill's house, Marcus pretended to bend down and do up his shoelace. He quickly pulled out the lipstick and smeared some on his lips. Then he stood up. His lips were tingling. He noticed that Jill was looking at him in a strange way; her eyes were wide open and staring. Then she rushed forward, threw her arms around Marcus's neck and kissed him. Marcus was so surprised that he nearly fell over.

Jill jumped back as if she had been burned. She put her hand up to her mouth and went red in the face. 'I, I, I'm sorry, Marcus. I don't know what came over me. What must you think of me? I've never done anything like that before.'

'Don't worry about it. That sort of thing happens to me all the time. The girls find me irresistible.'

Jill didn't know what to say. She was blushing. She couldn't understand what had happened. 'I'd better go

in,' she said. 'I'm really sorry. I didn't mean to do that.'
Then she turned around and rushed into the house.

Marcus whistled to himself as he walked home. 'It
works,' he thought. 'The lipstick really works.' He
couldn't wait to try it on someone else.

5

It was not so easy for Marcus to find his next victim.
None of the girls at school wanted to go out with him. It
was no use asking Jill again, as the lipstick only worked
once on each person. He asked ten girls to go to the
pictures with him and they all said 'no'.

He started to get cross. 'Stuck up snobs,' he said to
himself. 'I'll teach them a lesson.' He decided to make
the most popular girl in the school kiss him. That would
show them all. Her name was Fay Billings.

The trouble was that he knew she wouldn't go out on a
date with him. Then he had a bright idea: he wouldn't
even bother about a date. He would just go around to
Fay's house and ask to see her. He would put the lipstick
on before he arrived, and when she came to the door she
would give him a big kiss. The news would soon get
around and the other kids would think he had something
good going. It would make him popular with the girls.

Marcus grinned. It was a great idea. He decided to put
it into action straight away. He rode his bike around to
Fay's house and leaned it against the fence. Then he took
out the lipstick and put some on his lips. He walked up to
the front door and rang the bell with a big smile on his
face.

No one answered the door. He could hear a vacuum
cleaner going inside so he rang the bell again. The sound

of the vacuum cleaner stopped and Mrs Billings appeared at the door. She was about forty. She had a towel wrapped around her head and had dust on her face from the housework she had been doing. She had never seen Marcus before; he was not one of Fay's friends.

Mrs Billings was just going to ask Marcus what he wanted when a strange look came over her face. Her eyes went large and round. They looked as if they were going to pop out. Then she threw her arms around Marcus's neck and kissed him on the mouth.

It was hard to say who was more surprised, Marcus or Mrs Billings. They sprang apart and looked around to see if anyone had seen what happened. Marcus didn't want anyone to see him being kissed by a forty-year-old woman. How embarrassing. 'My goodness,' said Mrs Billings. 'What am I doing? Kissing a perfect stranger. And you're so young. What has got into me? What would my husband think? Please excuse me. I must be ill. I think I had better go and have a little rest.' She turned around and walked slowly into the house. She shook her head as she went.

6

Marcus rode home slowly. He was not pleased. This was not working out the way he wanted. What if someone had seen him being kissed by an old lady like Mrs Billings? He would never live it down. He had had the lipstick for two weeks now and had only received one decent kiss. None of the girls would go out with him. And he couldn't wear the lipstick just anywhere – he didn't want any other mothers kissing him.

He decided to make Fay Billings kiss him at school, in front of all the other kids. That would show them that he had something special. All the girls would be chasing him after that; He would be the most popular boy in the school.

He picked his moment carefully. He sat next to Fay for the Maths lesson the next day. She looked at him with a funny expression on her face but she didn't say anything. Miss White was late for the class. She was a young teacher and was popular with the students, but she was always late. This was the chance that Marcus had been waiting for. He bent down under the desk and put on some of the lipstick. Then he sat up in the desk and looked at Fay.

The lipstick worked. Fay's eyes went round and she threw herself onto Marcus and kissed him. Then she jumped back and gave a little cry. Marcus looked around with a grin on his face, but it did not last for long. All the girls' eyes were wide and staring. Tissy came up and kissed him. And then Gerda and Helen and Betty and Maria. They climbed over each other in the rush to get to him. They shrieked and screamed and fought; they scratched and fought and bit. Marcus fell onto the floor under a struggling, squirming heap of girls.

When all the sixteen girls in the class had kissed him there was silence. They were in a state of shock – they couldn't understand what had happened. They just sat there looking at each other. Marcus had his tie ripped off and his shirt was torn. He had a cut lip and a black eye.

Then Gerda yelled out, 'I kissed Marcus! Arrgghh . . .' She rushed over to the tap and started washing her mouth out. All the girls started wiping their mouths as if they had eaten something nasty. Then everybody started laughing. The boys laughed, and the girls laughed. They rolled around the floor holding their sides. Tears rolled out of their eyes. Everybody laughed, except Marcus.

He knew that they were laughing at him. And he didn't think that it was funny.

7

After all the kissing at school everyone called Marcus 'Lucky Lips'. Nobody liked Marcus any better than before and the girls still stayed away from him. Everyone talked about the kissing session for a while; then they forgot about it and talked about other things. But Marcus didn't forget about it. He felt like a fool. Everyone had laughed at him. He was worse off now than he had been before.

He thought about taking the lipstick back to Ma Scritchet and telling her what he thought about it, but he was too scared. There was something creepy about that old lady and he didn't really want to see her again.

Marcus didn't use the lipstick again for about a month. None of the girls would go out with him and he wasn't going to risk wearing it just anywhere. Not after what happened at school that day. But he always carried the lipstick with him, just in case.

The last time he used it was at the Royal Melbourne Show. The whole class at school went there on an excursion. They had to collect material for an assignment. Marcus and Fay Billings and two other boys walked around together. The others didn't really want Marcus with them; they thought he was a show off. But they let him tag along. They didn't want to hurt his feelings.

The favourite spots at the show were the sideshows. There were knock-em-downs and rides on the Mad Mouse. There was a fat lady and a mirror maze. There was a ghost train and dozens of other rides. One of the side shows had a sign up saying 'BIG BEN THE STRONGEST MAN IN THE WORLD'.

They all milled around looking at the tent. It was close to one of the animal pavilions. There was a great hall full of pigs nearby. 'Let's go and look at the pigs,' said Fay.

'No,' answered Marcus. 'Who wants to look at filthy pigs. Let's go and see Big Ben. He fights people. Anyone who can beat him wins one thousand dollars and gets to kiss the Queen Of The Show.'

'That would be just the thing for Lucky Lips,' said Fay. They all laughed, except Marcus. He went red in the face.

'I could get a kiss from the Queen Of The Show,' he said. They all laughed again. 'All right,' said Marcus. 'Just watch me.' He paid his dollar and went inside Big Ben's tent. The others all followed him; they wanted to see what was going to happen.

Inside the tent was a boxing ring. Big Ben was standing inside it waiting for someone to fight him and try to win the thousand dollars and a kiss from the Queen Of The Show. She sat on a high chair behind the ring. Marcus looked at her. She was beautiful; he wouldn't mind a kiss from her. Then he looked at Big Ben. He was the biggest man Marcus had ever seen. He had huge muscles and was covered in tattoos. And he looked mean – very mean.

49

Marcus ducked around the ring to where the Queen Of The Show sat. He quickly put on some of the invisible lipstick, and at once the beauty queen jumped off her chair and kissed Marcus. Everyone laughed except Big Ben. He roared in fury. 'Trying to steal a kiss without a fight, are you?' he yelled. 'I'll teach you a lesson, my boy.'

Marcus tried to run away but he was not quick enough. Big Ben grabbed him and lifted Marcus high into the air. Then he walked outside the tent and across to the pig pavilion. Marcus wriggled and yelled, but it was no good; he couldn't get away. Big Ben carried Marcus over to one of the pig pens and threw him inside.

Marcus crashed to the floor of the pen. He felt dizzy. The world seemed to be spinning around. He tried to stand up, but he couldn't. The floor was covered in foul smelling muck. In the corner Marcus could see the biggest pig that he had ever seen. It was eating rotten vegetables and slops from a trough. It was dribbling and slobbering as it ate. Its teeth were green. It turned around and looked at Marcus. It was a sow.

Marcus suddenly remembered something that Ma Scritchet had said about the lipstick. She had said: 'It will work on any female.' Marcus started to scream. 'Get me out. Get me out.'

But it was too late. The sow came over for her kiss.

COW DUNG CUSTARD

A lot of kids have nicknames. Like Mouse, or Bluey, or Freckles. Those sort of nicknames are okay. My nickname was the Cow Dung Kid. Can you imagine that? The Cow Dung Kid. What a name to get stuck with.

It was all my father's fault. Him and his vegetable garden.

Don't get me wrong, though. Dad was a good bloke. A real good bloke. He brought me up all on his own. I didn't have a mother so he can take all the credit for the way I turned out.

Dad loved to grow vegetables. His vegetable garden was his pride and joy. Every year he went into a competition. He always won lots of prizes for the best vegetables. He won prizes for the biggest pumpkins and the juiciest tomatoes. He grew the biggest and best vegies in the whole town. He once grew a pumpkin that was so big it took four men to lift it. His peas were as big as golf balls and his beans were as long as your arm. No kidding.

The whole yard was filled up with vegetables. He had

long rows of them. Every row had a little sign at the end. On each sign was the name of the vegetable that was growing. And the batch number. This batch number told which type of manure he had used.

Batch twenty-four meant three shovels of cow dung and one shovel of horse droppings. Batch fourteen was two shovels of horse droppings, one shovel of sheep droppings and three shovels of pig droppings.

Dad had every type of manure that you could think of. He had duck and goose. He had kangaroo and wombat. He had bat and emu. He even had snake droppings.

And guess who had to help him collect it. You are not wrong. It was me.

2

Every weekend I had to go and collect cow dung. Every weekend without fail. We lived right in the middle of the town. I had to get a wheelbarrow and walk out to the country. Then I had to fill it up with cow dung. And it had to be fresh. 'Nice and sloppy,' Dad would say. 'Make sure that it's nice and sloppy.'

Then I had to walk back through the town, with a wheelbarrow full of sloppy cow dung. I wasn't on my own, though. Oh no. I had company. About five thousand flies came with me. They were like a black cloud following me along the street.

Everyone could see me. It felt like the whole town was watching me and my flies.

I got my nickname of the Cow Dung Kid on one of these trips. It was on Christmas Day. Dad's boss at work grew vegetables too. But they were never as good as Dad's. He didn't have a son to go and get manure. So

Dad had a bright idea. He decided to give the boss a surprise. A Christmas present. He wanted me to go and get manure for his boss. 'Just tip it out and leave it for him to find,' said Dad. 'He will be tickled pink. I might even get a rise out of this.'

'But Dad,' I pleaded. 'Not on Christmas Day. Everyone will be looking. I can't do it. I just can't.'

He gave me one of his sorrowful looks. He shook his head and said, 'After all I've done for you, Greg. And you won't even help me out with one little thing.' I gave in and went. I didn't want to spend all Christmas feeling guilty.

I set out at the crack of dawn. I didn't even open my presents. I wanted to get it over and done with before people were out of bed.

But it was no use. All the kids in town were up early. They followed me and my cow dung along the street. They were all on new bikes and scooters that they had got for Christmas.

They thought it was a great joke. 'Look what Santa brought Greg,' shouted some bright spark. Everyone laughed. As I went along, more and more kids started following me. After a while there were about fifty of them.

Someone else yelled out, 'King Of The Flies. Greg is King of the flies.'

'The Cow Dung Kid,' said another voice. Another laugh went up. They all started yelling it out. 'Cow Dung Kid, Cow Dung Kid.' It was embarrassing, I can tell you that.

I ran faster and faster. Some of the cow dung fell out. But I didn't care. I just kept running. At last I reached the boss's house. I tipped out the cow dung on his doorstep. Right against the door. That way he would get a surprise when he opened the door. And Dad would get all the glory.

Anyway, that's how I got the name of the Cow Dung Kid. And after all that trouble Dad's boss wasn't even grateful. He said something about cow dung all over his carpet. There is just no understanding some people. He didn't even say thanks.

3

Flies, flies, flies. They hung around our house all day and all night. It was the smell of the manure. The smell attracted them. There were flies everywhere; they came down the chimney and under the doors. People had no trouble finding our house. If anyone asked where we lived they were always told the same thing. 'Just stop at the house with the flies.'

The neighbours didn't like the flies. They were always going crook. So Dad gave them vegetables to keep them quiet. He gave them giant carrots and potatoes. They liked them so much that they only complained about the really bad days. This usually happened when Dad made a very smelly batch, like batch seventy-two.

Dad kept each batch of manure in a large rubbish bin. He had at least two hundred of them in the back yard. The worse they smelt, the more flies hung around them. The ones with the really bad smell were kept down near the back fence, away from the house. Mr Farley lived in the house at the back. He didn't like us much – he never spoke to us. He was a pretty crabby bloke. I could never figure out why.

The trouble all started with batch seventy-two. It was the strongest batch that Dad had ever made. It had bat droppings, rabbit droppings and wombat droppings. There was also a bit of lizard and potaroo. But the main ingredient was cow dung.

Dad also threw in some rotten pumpkins. They were bright yellow. He added water and stirred the mix up. It all went smooth and yellow. 'It's like custard,' I said. 'Cow dung custard.'

It was a smelly batch, very smelly. It was the worst one that Dad had made. 'Good,' said Dad, 'The more it smells, the better it works. I'll grow some great potatoes with this batch.' He took out a pen and wrote Cow Dung Custard on the side of the bin. The flies were already starting to gather so I decided to go inside out of the way. The smell was bad and it was getting worse.

I could smell batch seventy-two as I went to bed, even though it was at the bottom of the yard. I knew there was going to be trouble with the neighbours over this. Batch seventy-two looked like custard. But it sure didn't smell like it.

4

The next morning I woke early. I knew that something was wrong. I could hardly breathe and I felt sick. It was the smell of the Cow Dung Custard. It was the most terrible smell I had ever come across. It was so bad that you could almost see it. Every breath was painful.

I put a handkerchief over my mouth and rushed to the window. All the neighbours were up. They were outside our house. Nobody could sleep. They were all dressed in their pyjamas, and they were all holding handkerchiefs over their noses. Some of them were making groaning noises. They were trying to shout. Some people were waving their fists at the house. They were all mad at us.

I went and woke Dad up. He has a poor sense of smell. He was the only person in the street who was still asleep. He looked out of the window. 'Amazing,' he said. 'Amazing. Look at that. There is not one fly to be seen.' He didn't even notice the people – he was looking for flies. I couldn't believe it. But what he said was true. There were no flies hanging around. They were all dead. The ground was covered in dead flies. They were like a black carpet all over the lawn.

The smell was so bad that it had killed all the flies. 'You had better do something,' I told him. 'That stuff might be dangerous. And everyone is mad at us. The neighbours are all angry.' He looked out of the window. Everyone was running away. The smell was so awful that they couldn't stand it.

'You're right,' said Dad. 'You stay here. I will go and see what I can do.' He walked down to the bottom of the yard. I could hear the bodies of the dead flies crunching under his feet. I was glad he had told me to stay inside. I think I would have fainted if I had gone any closer to that smell. It was lucky for Dad that he couldn't smell very well.

I watched him out of the window. He drove our old truck into the back yard. He tried to lift the cow dung custard onto it, but it was too heavy. He had to tip it out into a lot of buckets. Then he lifted them up onto the truck. After he had put all the buckets onto the truck he came back to the house. He had yellow stuff all over his dressing gown. 'Don't come in,' I shouted. 'Please don't come in.'

He yelled at me through the window. 'I'm going down to the sea with it. I can't think of anywhere else to put it. You stay here, Greg.' He needn't have worried. There was no way I was going anywhere near that Cow Dung Custard.

Then I noticed something terrible. Dad's hair had fallen out. He was completely bald. He did not have one hair left on his head – even his eyebrows had fallen out. That Cow Dung Custard was strong. Too strong.

Dad jumped into the truck and drove out the front gate. I watched him drive down the road. There wasn't a person in sight. They were all inside with their heads under their pillows. As he went by the dogs in the street ran off yelping with their tails between their legs.

5

Dad tipped the Cow Dung Custard over a cliff and into the sea. For the next two weeks there were dead fish floating around everywhere. The town we lived in is called Lakes Entrance. It is a fishing town. All the fisherman were cross with Dad, for killing the fish.

The people in the street were mad at him too. The smell hung around for weeks. Dad took a lot of vegetables around to them, trying to make it up. Mr Jackson lived next door. He told Dad to go away. 'I don't want your vegetables,' he said. 'And I don't want your manure, or your smells. Why don't you go and live out on a farm? Then you can be as smelly as you want.'

He had a point. I was getting sick of it too. The kids at school called me the Cow Dung Kid. Everyone knew us and where we lived. All the houses in the street had 'For Sale' notices in the front yard. No one wanted to live near us, and I didn't blame them.

'Listen, Dad,' I said. 'Let's go and live somewhere else – on a farm. Then I won't have to go and get manure. You will have all you want. And there won't be any neighbours to complain.'

Dad looked sad. He nodded his bald head. 'I would like to move to a farm, Greg. But we can't afford it. Farms cost a lot of money, and we're broke. We will have to stay here. But I will do one thing for you – I'll get rid of the smell. I'll find a way to stop the manure smelling. It will be called Batch One Hundred. Batch One Hundred will have no smell. And it's the only one I will use.'

I went off shaking my head. Poor old Dad. He meant well. But I knew he couldn't do it. How could anyone make up a batch of manure that didn't smell?

Dad tried everything he could think of to make Batch One Hundred. He put in flowers. He put in soap. He put in perfume. But he just couldn't stop the manure smelling.

Our house was as smelly as ever. Even the school bus wouldn't come down our street any more. One good thing did happen – Dad's hair started growing back. It was as thick and black as it had always been.

Then one day he did it. He made Batch One Hundred. You couldn't smell a thing. It wasn't like the Cow Dung Custard – you didn't even know it was there. I was rapt. I thought our problems were over.

But I was wrong. Batch One Hundred had other problems. It was the worst one ever.

6

People couldn't smell Batch One Hundred, but the flies could. Flies can smell better than people can. It's something like a dog whistle. Dogs can hear them and people can't. Well, flies could smell Batch One Hundred when people couldn't.

The flies came in their thousands. In their millions. The air was thick with them. The sound of their buzzling was terrible to hear. They crawled all over your face, and into your nose and ears. They were so thick that you couldn't see the sun. After a while it started to grow dark, and it was only lunch time.

Dad and I were in the back yard. After a while we couldn't even see the house, or the back fence. The flies were too thick. I had never seen anything like it before. There were so many flies in the air that I couldn't find Dad. 'Greg,' he shouted. 'Go back to the house. Quickly. This is dangerous.' I couldn't see where he was. I couldn't see where anything was.

I looked down at the ground. There were so many flies in the air that I couldn't see my feet. I had to squint to stop them getting into my eyes. I started to walk slowly to where I thought the house was. I bumped into something large. It was the truck. I could tell what it was by the feel of it. I was going the wrong way. I turned around and tried a different direction. Then I heard Dad's voice. I could just make it out over the buzzing of the flies. 'Greg, Greg, this way,' he called. I followed the sound of his voice. I walked very slowly to make sure I didn't bump into anything. At last I reached Dad. I couldn't see him but I could feel him. He was standing on the door step.

'Get ready,' he shouted. 'I'm going to open the door. When I say "go", rush in as quick as you can. I'll slam the door after us.'

'Go,' he yelled. We both fell into the room. I couldn't see anything but I heard the door shut with a bang. 'Put on the light,' said Dad.

I switched on the light. The room was full of flies, but it wasn't as bad as outside. At least we could see. I looked at the window. It was black. Millions of flies were crawling all over it. 'Quick,' said Dad. 'Block up all the cracks under the doors. I'll cover up the chimney. We've got to stop them coming in.'

I started stuffing towels and rags under the door. Dad covered up the fireplace with a piece of cardboard. When we had all the cracks blocked up he found some fly spray. We had plenty of fly spray in the house – it was something we used a lot of. It took three cans to kill them all.

We ran upstairs to look out of the top windows. They were all black too. We couldn't see outside at all. We were trapped in our own house by millions and millions of flies.

7

Dad was upset. 'This is bad, Greg,' he said. 'Very bad. Batch One Hundred is much too strong. Every fly in the country must be here, and it's all my fault. We've got to get rid of those flies.'

Just then the phone rang. Dad picked it up. It was Mr Jackson. He was shouting. I could hear every word even though the flies were making such a loud noise outside. 'You've done it this time, Moffit,' he yelled. 'The whole town is blacked out with flies. Nobody can get out of their house. It's pitch black in the middle of the day. It's all your fault, you and your manure. You'd better do something, and quick. You brought the flies here. Now you get rid of them.' The phone went dead. He had hung up.

'What can we do?' said Dad. 'How can we get rid of them?' He hung his head in his hands. The poor bloke – I really felt sorry for him. We both sat there thinking. Outside the flies were getting thicker and thicker.

'Fly spray,' I said.

'No good,' he told me. 'There isn't enough fly spray in the world to kill this lot. We need something stronger. Something really powerful.'

We sat there looking at each other. We both thought of the answer at the same time. 'Cow Dung Custard,' we shouted together.

'That's it,' said Dad. 'The smell is so strong that it kills flies. I'll mix up a special batch.'

'But what about the smell, Dad?' I asked.

'We can't help the smell. This is an emergency. The whole town is blacked out with flies. We have to do something.'

'But how can we make it?' I asked him. 'You can't see a thing out there. You can hardly breathe. The flies get into your nose and mouth. You wouldn't be able to make the Cow Dung Custard. It's as black as pitch.'

We both fell silent again. We just sat and looked at each other. Then Dad had an idea. 'The bee-keeper's outfit,' he yelled. 'I can wear the bee-keeper's outfit.' Once Dad used to keep bees. He still had the outfit for smoking out the bees. It had a hat and net to stop the bees from stinging him.

'What about me? You can't do it on your own. You'll have to make a heck of a lot. I'll have to come too.'

'Your wet suit. You can wear your wet suit. And put on the goggles. You can wear the snorkel to stop the flies getting into your mouth.'

We dressed up in our outfits. Dad had his hat and bee net. I had my wet suit, goggles and snorkel. I felt silly. But, as Dad said, this was an emergency. We tied a rope to each other so that we didn't become lost. Then we walked over to the door and opened it.

8

A million flies poured into the room. Everything went black. The light was on but we couldn't even see it. I felt a pull on the rope. Dad was moving out into the back yard. I couldn't see him so I just follwed the rope. The flies swirled around us in one huge, black cloud.

We walked slowly. We didn't want to fall over. At last we reached the back fence. I felt Dad's hand on my arm. He was shouting at me. It was difficult to hear him because of the loud buzzing of the flies. 'Help me tip over Batch One Hundred,' he yelled. 'Then we will empty another fifteen bins. We will need at least sixteen bins of Cow Dung Custard to kill all these flies. They must be covering the whole town.'

We struggled over to Batch One Hundred. The flies were all trying to get to it. They were so thick that it was like walking through a river. I plunged my arm through the sea of flies and pushed over the bin. A billion flies rose into the air as it tipped over. The buzz was so loud that it hurt my ears, and the wind from their wings blew me over.

We stood up and felt our way to the other bins. It took a long time to push them all over and empty out the manure. In the end we had sixteen empty bins. I felt Dad's hand on my arm again. 'We will have to untie the rope,' he shouted. 'It will take a long time to mix up sixteen bins of Cow Dung Custard. We have to hurry. The flies are getting thicker. Every fly in Australia will be here soon.'

'I'm scared, Dad,' I told him. 'I might get lost if you untie the rope.'

'Feel your way along the fence,' he said. 'When you get to the manure heap try to fill up the wheelbarrow with cow dung. Put ten shovels full into each bin. I'll put in the rest of the mixture.' His voice was shaking; I knew that he was scared too. So I undid the rope and followed the fence to the manure heap.

It took a long time, but at last I managed to put cow dung in every bin. The flies kept bumping into my goggles – it felt as if someone was throwing rice at me. Every now and then I bumped into Dad. He was tipping all sorts of things into the bins. Once he dropped a rotten pumpkin onto my foot.

Then something wonderful happened. A shocking stink filled the air. It was the first batch of Cow Dung Custard. 'Hooray,' I shouted. I was really happy even though the smell was so bad. I didn't know whether it was working. I couldn't tell if it was killing the flies. There seemed to be just as many as ever.

Dad came over to me. 'Go back to the house,' he yelled. 'If this works there are going to be dead flies everywhere. You might get buried if you stay here.'

'No way,' I told him. 'I'm staying with you.'

9

After a while we had two bins of Cow Dung Custard mixed up. The stink grew stronger and stronger. I felt ill, but I had to keep going. We made one bin at a time. By the time we had made ten bins the smell was so strong we had to stop.

'We can't go on,' said Dad. 'I'm going to faint, if I don't get away from this smell.'

'Hey!' I suddenly shouted. 'I can see you.' I could just make out the shape of Dad in his bee net. There were not so many flies in the air. The Cow Dung Custard was working – it was killing some of the flies.

I looked at the ground. It was covered in flies. Some of them were dead, and some were lying on their backs kicking their legs in the air. There was a thick carpet of flies all over the lawn. Then I felt my head. My hair was full of dead flies. They were starting to fall down out of the sky. It was raining flies.

'Quick,' said Dad. 'Back to the house. We will be buried alive if we don't hurry.'

We ran back to the house. Flies were pouring down all around us. The dead bodies were so deep that we couldn't move properly. They came up to my ankles and then up to my knees. Dad reached the door first. He pushed it open and fell inside.

'Help!' I screamed. 'I'm stuck.' The flies were up to my arm pits and they were still falling. I was scared out of my wits. I didn't want to drown in a sea of flies. I couldn't move backwards or forwards.

Dad still had the rope wrapped around his waist. He started to undo it. 'Quick, I'm going under,' I yelled. The flies were getting deeper and deeper – they were nearly up to my mouth. He threw the rope over and I grabbed the end of it. But it was too late. The dead flies were right over my head. I was buried under the bodies of the flies.

It was lucky that I had the goggles and snorkel on. The snorkel poked above the pile of flies. It enabled me to breathe, but I couldn't see a thing. Everything was black. Then I felt strong hands pulling me up. It was Dad. He had followed the rope and dug down to me. He dragged me across the top of the flies and into the house. Then he slammed the door.

10

It was much better in the house. The flies were only knee deep. At least we could walk around. We went upstairs as quickly as we could and looked out of the window. It was still raining flies, but it was starting to ease off. At last it stopped. Every fly was dead. The Cow Dung Custard had killed the lot. The smell of it was terrible.

Our place was on the top of a hill. We could see the whole town. Every house was covered in dead flies. They covered the road and the cars, the trees and the gardens. It looked just like a snow-covered village, but with black snow. There was not a person in sight. Everyone was trapped inside their houses. The whole town was silent. And over it hung the terrible smell of Cow Dung Custard.

Dad looked at me. 'Good grief, Greg,' he said. 'All of your hair has gone.'

I felt the top of my head. It was smooth. I was as bald as a badger. I rushed to the mirror. 'Oh no,' I groaned. 'Not that. Not bald.' Then I looked at Dad. He was bald again too. All of his new hair had fallen out.

'It's the Cow Dung Custard,' I said. 'It's so strong that it makes hair fall out.'

I looked out of the window again. It was still very quiet, but four or five people were out. They were trying to clear the flies away from their front doors. It was hard work – they were up to their armpits in flies. I looked at them more closely. There was something strange about them but I couldn't work out what it was. Then I got a shock. They were all bald. I knew there was going to be big trouble over this.

A bit later we heard the sound of a motor. It sounded like a tractor, but it wasn't. It was a bulldozer. It was clearing the streets. It pushed the flies to the side of the road in huge banks. Behind the bulldozer was a police car. They came slowly up our street. People were following them, lots of bald people. Men, women and children. They were angry. They were mad. They were yelling and screaming at us.

The bulldozer stopped at our house. It turned around and came through our garden. It cleared a path up to the front door; then it stopped. A bald policeman stepped down from it. He had a handkerchief tied around his nose to stop the smell. He came into the house without knocking. 'Quick,' he said. 'Get into the police car. I'll have to get you out of here before the mob gets you. I don't know what they will do if they get their hands on you. They might tear you to pieces.' He was worried – very worried. So was I.

He pushed us into the car and started driving down the street. Crowds of bald people surrounded the car. They threw things at the car and tried to open the doors. They wanted to pull us out. Some even threw handfuls of flies at the car.

I could see why they were mad. Everyone was bald, even the dogs and cats. Not one person in the town had a hair left anywhere on their body.

In the end the police got us safely through the town. They took us down to Melbourne, which was a long way away. Then they let us go. Dad and I were both upset. We knew one thing for sure – we could never go back to Lakes Entrance again.

11

There was a big fuss about the whole thing. It was in all the papers and on the TV. Dad and I changed our names so that nobody could find us. Then it all died down and people started to forget about it. There was a shortage of wigs in Australia for a while. But after a couple of months everybody's hair grew back. As time passed people started to think it was funny.

I'm writing this next to the swimming pool on our farm. Dad is out the front cleaning our Rolls Royce. Things worked out quite well for us in the end. Dad made a lot of money out of an invention. It's yellow stuff for getting rid of hair. People buy it in tubes. They put it on their legs. It works really well and it smells lovely.

It's called CDC Hair Remover. Everybody likes it. They think it's wonderful. But nobody knows what CDC stands for.

LIGHTHOUSE BLUES

Someone was playing music in the middle of the night. It sounded like a saxophone, or maybe a clarinet. I could only hear it when the wind dropped. But there was no mistake about it.

I shivered even though I was snug in bed. I wasn't cold. I was scared. Stan and I were the only people on the island, and he was in bed in the next room. I could hear him snoring. So who was playing the music?

It was cold outside and a storm was brewing up. I could hear the sea pounding against the cliffs. I got out of bed and looked out of the window. All I could see was the black clouds racing across the moon, and the light from the lighthouse stabbing into the night. The music seemed to be coming from the lighthouse.

I thought about waking Stan up, but I decided not to. He was the lighthouse keeper. He was a nice old boy but I didn't want him to think I was scared. I was hoping to get a job as a lighthouse keeper myself one day. This was my first night on the island and I wanted to make a good impression.

I climbed back into bed and tried to get to sleep. I tried not to listen to the music. It was soft and far away, but it crept into my brain. It was like a soft voice calling to me. It was saying something; it was speaking without words. I knew I had heard the tune before, but I couldn't think what it was. It was a slow and haunting tune. Then it came to me. I remembered. It was called 'Stranger On The Shore'.

Somehow I knew that the music was meant for me. I was the stranger. I had just arrived on the island. The supply boat had dropped me on the shore that very day. But who was playing the music? And why did it make me feel so sad?

I listened more carefully. It was a clarinet. It was definitely a clarinet. And man, I will tell you this. Whoever was blowing it knew how to play. It was the saddest and most beautiful music I have ever heard.

Then the music changed. There was something different about it. Finally I realised what it was – another instrument had joined in. It was a saxophone. They were both playing 'Stranger On The Shore'. It was so sad that I felt like crying, but I didn't know why.

After a long time I fell asleep with the music still sounding in my ears.

2

The next morning at breakfast I asked Stan if he had heard anything. 'No, Anton,' he said. 'I didn't hear anything. I never do. But I know there is something there. Visitors to the island always hear it. Most people can't stand it. They get scared and leave. You are the third helper that I have had here this year. The other two left because of the music. They said it kept them awake at night. But the real reason was because they were scared – scared out of their wits.'

He looked straight at me when he said this. He was wondering if I was going to run off too. He glared at me with his one eye. He had a patch over the other one. He looked like a fierce pirate, but he was really a friendly bloke. He loved that island more than anything in the world.

'Well, who could be playing the music?' I asked him. 'And why can't you hear it?'

He looked at me for a long time. He looked straight into my eyes, as if he was trying to see what I was thinking. Then he said, 'The last boy went up to the lighthouse one Friday night. The music always plays on Friday night. He took a torch and went off to see who was playing. He was gone for two hours. When he came back he wouldn't say anything about it. He just said that he was leaving. He wouldn't speak to me. He wouldn't answer any questions at all. He just sat in here and looked at the wall. A week later the supply boat came and he left.'

'He must have seen something terrible,' I said. 'Don't you have any idea who could be playing?'

'Put on your coat, boy,' Stan said, 'and come with me. I'll show you something.'

A strong wind was blowing. It was coming from the south west. Stan took me along a track which ran along the top of the rocky cliffs. There were no trees; the wind was too strong for trees to grow on the island. At last we came to a small fence in the shape of a square. Inside were two graves. The headstones faced out to sea. It was a lonely, windswept spot, high on the cliff.

We opened a small gate and went inside the cemetery. I looked at the headstones. The first one was engraved like this:

CAPTAIN RICKARD

1895-1950

LIGHTHOUSE KEEPER FROM

1915-1950

R.I.P.

The second gravestone was not much different, but it had another name on it. It said:

ALAN RICKARD

1915-1960

LIGHTHOUSE KEEPER FROM

1950-1960

R.I.P.

Stan pointed to the grave of Captain Rickard. 'He was my grandfather,' he said. 'And Alan Rickard was my father.'

Both gravestones had a small drawing in the corner. The one of Captain Rickard had a clarinet. Alan Rickard's grave had a saxophone.

'All the lighthouse keepers have been musical,' said Stan. 'The Captain played the clarinet. And my father played the saxophone. I play the violin. Do you play anything, boy?'

'Yes,' I replied. 'I play the flute.'

3

Stan and I walked slowly back to the house. The wind was blowing strongly. It flattened the grass and made my hair whip into my eyes. Stan had to shout so that I could hear.

'I can't play the violin any more,' he told me. 'My fingers won't work properly. I have arthritis. The violin is in the music room at the top of the lighthouse. My grandfather and father used to play up there when they were alive. It was something to do when they were on duty. I don't go in there anymore; I can't bear to look at my violin.'

Stan's eye was wet. Perhaps the wind was doing it. Or was he crying?

We walked back to the house without speaking. I didn't know what to think. Did the two graves have anything to do with that sad music? The dead captain had played the clarinet. And his son had played the saxophone. But they were dead, and dead men play no tunes. Or that's what I thought.

One day I decided that I would go up to the top of the lighthouse. I might find some clues. But I was not going to go in the night time. Nor was I going to go on a Friday.

The next day was Thursday. I told Stan I was going for a walk to look around the island, but I went to the lighthouse. I had been there before. Stan had taken me up on the first day. I had been in and seen the huge light that went around and around at night. But I had not been in the music room, and I had not been up there on my own.

I pushed open the door at the bottom and went in. It

was gloomy inside. There were small windows in the wall and they let in a little bit of light. The stairs went around and around. Stan had told me that there were twenty turns altogether. I went slowly up the stairs. It was as quiet as a grave. About half way up I looked over the side of the stairs. It was a long way down; I felt giddy. I sat down on a step and listened. Nothing. Not a sound. I was sure that I was alone.

At last I reached the top. There were two doors. One led into the light; the other was the door of the music room. I tried the handle. It was stiff, but it opened, and I stepped inside. The room looked like a cabin in a ship. It had bunks against one wall and maps all over another. There was a desk with a globe of the world on it. Instead of a window there was a small, round porthole. Pointing out of the porthole was a telescope. There was a music stand and a small table. On the table was a clarinet, a saxophone and a violin.

I went and looked at the musical instruments. They were covered in dust; they had not been played for a long time. The violin had a spider's web inside it. I picked up the clarinet and blew it. A terrible noise came out of it – it sounded like a bullfrog choking.

These instruments could not have been playing on Friday night.

They had not been played for years. I had not got any closer to solving the mystery, but I knew that the music had been coming from that room. I could feel it in my bones.

I decided to leave. There was something creepy about the room. I felt as if someone was watching me.

Over the next few months I was kept very busy on the island. I had to measure the rainfall and record the weather. I had to man the radio and listen for ships that were in trouble. And every night at five o'clock I had to climb the stairs of the lighthouse and start up the light. I didn't go into the music room, and I didn't say any more to Stan about the music.

But every Friday at about midnight the music would start. It was always sad, haunting music. I could never sleep while it was playing. It seemed to be calling me. The names of the tunes always seemed to have a special meaning – a meaning just meant for me.

It was upsetting. I wasn't scared any more, but I couldn't sleep on Friday nights. I just lay there waiting for the music to start. And then I lay awake waiting for it to stop. I couldn't stop thinking about it. I wondered who was playing and why.

In the end I decided to go and see. I made my plans carefully. I decided not to tell Stan. I put fresh batteries in the torch and found an old baseball bat. The baseball bat was in case there was any trouble. The next Friday I waited until Stan was in bed asleep; then I stepped out of the house and into the dark night.

It was cold and windy. The moon was hidden behind black clouds. Spray was blowing up from the sea and the waves were crashing and sucking beneath the cliffs. In the distance I could hear music. It was coming from the lighthouse. I walked slowly, fighting against the wind. At last I reached the lighthouse door.

It was dark inside. There was no light in the stair well. But music was floating down from above. I had heard the tune before. It was 'Stay Away From Me Baby'. I knew it was meant for me. But who was up there? And why didn't they like strangers on the island? I was scared – I didn't want to go up. But I forced myself. My knees were knocking together as I climbed the dark stairs.

I went around and around. I was glad that I had my torch – it was creepy in there. The music echoed. It seemed to be laughing at me. 'You won't get rid of me,' I said aloud. 'You won't scare me off like the others.' I tried to sound tough, but I didn't feel tough. I wanted to turn round and run back to the house. I forced my legs to take me all the way to the top.

There was light coming under the music room door. The music was very loud. It was definitely coming from the music room. Suddenly the tune changed. Now they were playing 'The Green Door'. I thought of some of the words. They were: 'What's behind the green door?' The door of the music room was green, and I wanted to know what was behind it. But I was too scared to go in. Whatever was in there knew where I was. Then the door started to open on its own. It just slowly opened.

I couldn't believe what I saw. I started shaking all over. The hair on the back of my neck stood up. I wanted to turn around and run, but I couldn't. My legs wouldn't do what I wanted them to. The clarinet was playing itself. And the saxophone was doing the same thing. They were both floating in mid-air. Someone or something was playing them, but they were invisible.

I was really scared. My knees were knocking together. I decided to get out of there. Then I thought about the other two boys who had left the island. I wasn't going to be scared off like them – no fear! No ghosts were going to chase me away. I took a step forward into the room.

As soon as I entered the room the music stopped. The

clarinet and the saxophone floated through the air and landed on the table. Everything was quiet. I went over to the table and picked up the clarinet. It was covered in cobwebs; it looked as if it had not been played in years. I picked it up and blew in it. A cloud of dust came out of the end.

5

Something had been blowing those musical instruments only moments before, and now they were covered in dust. Ghosts. It had to be ghosts. The ghosts of Captain Rickard and Alan Rickard. Stan's father and grandfather. But why were they so unhappy? And why did they want to scare away everyone who came to the island?

I decided to talk to them. I was still scared. I had never met any ghosts before. But it was worth a try. 'Listen, guys,' I said. 'What's the matter? What are you trying to scare me away for? I won't hurt you, or the island. I won't even touch anything in this room. Come out and show yourselves.'

Nothing happened. The room was empty and quiet; I could hear myself breathing. Then I started to feel cold all over. I started to shiver. They were in the room with me but they wouldn't answer. I felt as if cold, cold hands were touching me. Cold hands from the grave. I let out a scream and ran for my life. I tore down the stairs and ran out into the dark night.

As I ran back to the house the music started up again. They were playing 'See You Later Alligator'. I knew they were laughing at me. They thought they had scared me off, but they were wrong. I was scared all right, but I wasn't leaving. No way.

I got back to the house and went into the kitchen. Stan was sitting at the table with his head in his hands. He looked up at me as I came in. I could see that he had been crying; he had been rubbing his one eye and his cheek was wet.

'I've just had a radio message,' he said. 'They are going to pull down the lighthouse.'

'Who is?'

'The people in charge. The government. They have been talking about it for years, but I didn't think they would really do it. They are going to put in a lighthouse that doesn't need a keeper. An automatic one. It will just be a tall tower with a light on the top.'

My mouth fell open. Stan would be out of a job and so would I. We would have to leave the island. 'They just can't do it,' I said. 'They just can't.'

'Yes, they can,' said Stan. 'They are coming next Friday. We are supposed to help them knock down the lighthouse.' He looked very old. He didn't know what to do. He just sat there shaking his head and staring into the fire. After a while he spoke again. 'My father died here. And my grandfather. I wanted to spend my last days here too. Now I will have to go and live on the mainland. They will probably put me in an old folk's home.'

Suddenly I had an idea. 'Wait a minute. Don't give up yet, Stan. We're not the only ones on this island, you know. We can get some help. We can put up a fight to save the lighthouse.'

Stan looked up at me sadly. He didn't know what I was talking about.

6

I thought I knew why the music was playing. The two ghosts lived in the lighthouse. They didn't want it to be knocked down. So they played spooky music every time a stranger came to the island – they tried to scare them off. They didn't care about Stan. He was their grandson and he loved the island. They knew he wouldn't hurt the lighthouse. That's why he never heard the music.

But playing music on Friday nights wouldn't work, not against the wreckers. They would come in the daytime. And it would only take one day to knock down the lighthouse. Then it would be gone for ever. It would be too late to do anything then.

I had to talk to the ghosts. I had to tell them that I was friendly, that I didn't want the lighthouse to be knocked down, and that I needed their help to save it.

I ran out of the house and up to the music room. It was as quiet as death. The saxophone and clarinet lay on the table. I didn't waste any time. 'Listen, guys,' I said. 'I know you are here. And I know you can hear me. I want you to show yourselves. I'm your friend; I want to help you. I don't want the lighthouse to be knocked down. I want to save it. But I need your help.'

Nothing happened. There was dead silence. I felt a bit silly. Maybe I was talking to myself. Maybe there weren't any ghosts. Had I dreamed it all? Was I going mad? Then I looked at the clarinet and saxophone. I knew I had heard them playing. I started to get angry.

'You stupid ghosts,' I shouted. 'Don't you know that this place is going to be knocked down? The wreckers are coming on Friday. We have to stop them. Stan and I need your help. Playing music on Friday nights won't stop them. We have to think of something else.'

Silence. If the ghosts were there they weren't saying anything. 'Okay,' I yelled. 'Have it your own way. Let them knock down the lighthouse. Let them throw poor old Stan out of a job. You won't have any home. You will just be blown around by the wind.'

When I said this I noticed something happen. Some drops of water were slowly dribbling through the air. They looked like raindrops running down a piece of glass. But there was no glass there. There were two lots of them trickling downwards. At first I felt frightened, but then I realised what they were. They were tears – teardrops running down invisible faces. The ghosts were crying.

7

I knew I had won. The ghosts were on my side; they didn't want the lighthouse to be knocked down. But they still weren't saying anything. Then I realised why. They couldn't talk. Ghosts can't talk.

'Look,' I said. 'This is no good. I can't see you and I can't hear you. I want you to pick up the musical instruments if you are going to help.'

Very slowly the clarinet and the saxophone started to rise in the air. As they did so the dust and cobwebs fell off. They were sparkling like new. Then they started to play. I recognised the tune straight away. It was 'We Shall Not Be Moved'.

'That's the spirit,' I said. 'Now you will have to come outside. We need you to scare the wreckers off. You will have to come outside to do that. In the daytime. In broad daylight.'

The music stopped. The clarinet and the saxophone started waggling from side to side. The ghosts didn't want to go outside. 'It's no good doing that,' I said. 'You will have to come outside. You will have to scare the wreckers off before they get to the lighthouse. They might blow it up with dynamite from the outside. A bit of music at midnight won't do the trick. Come on. Come with me now, before they get here. You can practise going out in the daytime.'

I walked out of the room and started going down the stairs. Half way down I looked over my shoulder to see if they were coming. They were. The saxophone and the clarinet were slowly floating down the staircase. They were bobbing up and down as they went. I couldn't see the ghosts. 'Hang on to those musical instruments,' I told them. 'It's the only way I know where you are.'

When we got to the bottom I looked outside. The wind was blowing a little bit. It was not very strong, only a breeze. I stepped outside and turned around. 'Come on, you two,' I said. 'There is nothing out here to hurt you.'

I was wrong about that, but I didn't know it at the time. They started waggling again. They didn't want to come out. I waved my arms at them. 'Don't you want to save the lighthouse?'

The clarinet and the saxophone slowly floated outside. Then something terrible happened – they started to blow off in the wind. The wind was blowing the ghosts away. They were drifting off towards the edge of the cliff. I ran over to the clarinet and tried to grab it. My fingers went right through it; it wasn't solid. When the ghosts touched the musical instruments they changed. They became ghostly. I tried to grab the saxophone, but the same thing happened. There was nothing I could do to help.

They drifted closer and closer to the edge. Then both instruments fell to the ground. They started to slowly move along the ground in little jumps. I knew what was happening. The ghosts were crawling. They were trying to crawl back to the lighthouse by hanging on to the grass. The wind started to blow more strongly. I was worried that they might blow out to sea. 'Come on,' I shouted. 'You can do it. Keep going. Keep going.'

And they did keep going. All I could see was a saxophone and a clarinet making small hops across the ground. It took a long time, but at last they got back to the lighthouse. They went inside. I tried to go after them but the door slammed in my face. I opened the door and was just in time to see the instruments floating quickly up the stairs.

When I got up to the music room everything was quiet. The instruments were on the table, covered in cobwebs. And the ghosts were nowhere to be seen. 'Come on, guys,' I said. 'I'm sorry. I didn't know the wind would blow you away. Come back. We will think of something else.'

But there was no answer. They were mad at me. And I didn't blame them. After all, I had nearly got them killed, if you know what I mean.

8

I told Stan about what had happened. He believed me. I didn't think he would; I could hardly believe it myself. 'Yes,' he said. 'I knew something was up there. I thought that it might be Captain Rickard and my dear old dad. But I didn't really know. I have never heard them myself.'

'What are we going to do?' I asked him. 'How are we going to stop the wreckers? The ghosts won't help us now. They are mad at me.'

Stan shook his head sadly. 'I don't see what they could do anyway,' he said. 'If they can't come outside they won't be much use to us. We'll just have to try and stop the wreckers on our own.'

I went up the music room every day that week. I begged and I pleaded. But nothing happened; the room was empty and cold. There was no sign of the ghosts. I didn't know whether they could hear me or not.

At last Friday came. A ship arrived at first light. It unloaded five men and a bulldozer. There was also a tall crane with a huge steel ball on the end. I knew what that was for – it was to knock the lighthouse down. The men set up camp down by the beach.

Stan and I watched them from the house. 'I'm going down to see them,' said Stan. 'You wait here. I don't want you losing your temper. Let me handle it. I'll ask them to go away. I'll tell them that we are not going to help.'

'That won't do any good,' I said. 'They won't take any notice. It's no good talking. We will have to sit down in front of the bulldozer or something like that.'

'First I will try talking,' said Stan. 'It's worth a try.'

I watched him walk down to the beach. He was bent over and he walked slowly. His white beard was flapping in the wind. A strong south westerly was blowing. I saw him talking to the men – he was pointing to the light-house and shaking his head. One of the men started waving his fists at Stan. I could see that they were shouting at each other. Stan turned around and came back to the house.

'It's no use,' he said as he came in the door. 'They won't listen. They said they have a job to do. They have given us until lunch time to get all our things out of the lighthouse. Then they are going to knock it down. The only thing I want is my violin,' he said. 'Not that I can play it any more – not with these old hands. Go and get it for me, will you, boy?'

I went up to the music room and picked up the old violin. I decided to leave the clarinet and the saxophone. They belonged to the ghosts. I decided to talk to them once more. 'Listen, ghosts,' I said. 'I'm really sorry that you were blown away in the wind. It's windy today so I know you can't go outside. But you must be able to do something. We need your help. Stan is too old. He can't do much to stop the wreckers. They are going to knock the lighthouse down this afternoon.' I waited a long time. But there was no answer. In the end I turned around and walked away. Stan and I were on our own.

9

After lunch the bulldozer and the crane started up towards the lighthouse. There was a very narrow part where the track went close to the edge of the cliff. The bulldozer and the crane would have to go past there.

Stan and I sat down on the track. We held hands and waited. 'I hope they don't run over us,' I said to Stan.

'They won't,' he replied, but he didn't sound too sure.

It didn't take long for the bulldozer to reach us. Its big steel blade stopped just in front of our faces. The driver got down. 'Get out of the way,' he said, 'or I'll squash you flat.'

'No,' said Stan. 'We're not moving.' His voice was shaking.

I looked up at the driver. He was an ugly looking brute, and he was big. Very big. He picked Stan up with one hand and threw him out of the way. Stan landed on the ground with a thump. He didn't move. He looked as if he was hurt.

'Leave him alone,' I screamed. 'He is an old man. Leave him alone.'

The driver gave an ugly grin. 'Now it's your turn,' he said. He picked me up the same way. I kicked and struggled but it was no good. He threw me out of the way. Three other men came and held me down. The bulldozer and the crane moved up towards the lighthouse. The crane stopped right in front of the lighthouse door. The big steel ball started to swing backwards and forwards through the air.

Then I noticed something. The wind had stopped blowing. It was very still. I listened carefully. Yes, I could hear music. The door of the lighthouse opened and out came the clarinet and the saxophone. They were playing 'When The Saints Come Marching In'.

The driver of the crane couldn't believe what he was seeing. His eyes nearly popped out of his head. A saxophone and a clarinet were floating through the air and playing a tune. He jumped off the crane and ran down the track. He was screaming his head off.

The saxophone floated up above the seat of the crane. The crane started moving backwards towards the sea. One of the ghosts had put it into reverse gear. It rumbled slowly towards the cliff. The ghost was still sitting on it. I could see the saxophone – it was still over the driver's seat. Then the crane started to tumble over the cliff. At the last minute the ghost jumped clear. The saxophone came floating back.

The driver of the bulldozer let out a roar. He put the blade up and drove towards the lighthouse. Stan jumped up and pulled one of the levers. The bulldozer turned and headed towards the cliff. Stan and the driver were both stuggling over the controls. The bulldozer got closer and closer to the edge. The driver suddenly jumped off. Stan tried to jump off too, but his leg was stuck. The bulldozer tipped over the edge and fell. Down, down, down it went. And Stan went with it. It tumbled over and over. And then it crashed on the rocks beneath.

The ghosts stared playing louder and louder. It wasn't a tune, it was a loud roaring noise. It was angry and sad at the same time. Then both instruments fell to the ground. I didn't know where the ghosts were. Then I saw the driver rise up into the air. The ghosts were lifting him up. They suddenly dropped him. He fell onto his head. He let out a scream and started running down the track. The other men followed him. They were scared to death.

I went and looked over the edge of the cliff. The two ghosts picked up their instruments and stood next to me.

I couldn't see them. I could just see the saxophone and the clarinet floating in the air. I knew that Stan was dead. No one would have lived through that crash.

The ghosts started playing a sad, sad tune. I knew the first lines. They were: 'We'll meet again. Don't know where, don't know when. But I know we'll meet again some sunny day.'

I looked at the grey sea. The wind was blowing the spray high into the air.

The wind.

'Quick,' I yelled. 'Back to the lighthouse. The wind is getting up.' But I was too late. A sudden gust of wind blew both ghosts over the edge and out to sea. I watched as the clarinet and the saxophone drifted away, getting smaller and smaller. They looked like two tiny leaves blowing along in a storm. In the end I couldn't see them any more; they were gone.

10

Well, that is just about the end of the story. Stan was buried in the tiny cemetery next to the other two graves. The wreckers left and didn't come back. Their union said that the men would not work on the island. They said it was too dangerous.

I was made lighthouse keeper. I have been here for a year now. I love the island; I hope I can always stay here. But it gets very lonely. I often wish that Stan was still alive.

Last night something happened. Something good. It was Friday. I was just closing my eyes when I thought I heard music. It was coming from the lighthouse. I jumped out of bed and ran as fast as I could. I stopped when I reached the music room door. It was a saxo-phone and a clarinet. But something was different. I pushed open the door a tiny bit and peeped in. The clarinet and the saxophone were floating in the air as usual. But there was another instrument as well. It was a violin. It looked as if it was playing itself. But I knew that Stan was playing it. There were three ghosts now.

I smiled to myself and closed the door. As I walked back down the stairs I hummed a tune to myself. I knew the song well. It was 'Happy Days Are Here Again'.

SMART ICE CREAM

Well, I came top of the class again. One hundred out of one hundred for Maths. And one hundred out of one hundred for English. I'm just a natural brain, the best there is. There isn't one kid in the class who can come near me. Next to me they are all dumb.

Even when I was a baby I was smart. The day that I was born my mother started tickling me. 'Bub, bub bub,' she said.

'Cut it out, Mum,' I told her. 'That tickles.' She nearly fell out of bed when I said that. I was very advanced for my age.

Every year I win a lot of prizes: top of the class, top of the school, stuff like that. I won a prize for spelling when I was only three years old. I am a terrific speller. If you can say it, I can spell it. Nobody can trick me on spelling. I can spell every word there is.

Some kids don't like me; I know that for a fact. They say I'm a show off. I don't care. They are just jealous because they are not as clever as me. I'm good looking too. That's another reason why they are jealous.

Last week something bad happened. Another kid got one hundred out of one hundred for Maths too. That never happened before – no one has ever done as well as me. I am always first on my own. A kid called Jerome Dadian beat me. He must have cheated. I was sure he cheated. It had something to do with that ice-cream. I was sure of it. I decided to find out what was going on; I wasn't going to let anyone pull a fast one on me.

It all started with the ice-cream man. Mr Peppi. The old fool had a van which he parked outside the school. He sold ice-cream, all different types. He had every flavour there is, and some that I had never heard of before.

He didn't like me very much. He told me off once. 'Go to the back of the queue,' he said. 'You pushed in.'

'Mind your own business, Pop,' I told him. 'Just hand over the ice cream.'

'No,' he said. 'I won't serve you unless you go to the back.'

I went round to the back of the van, but I didn't get in the queue. I took out a nail and made a long scratch on his rotten old van. He had just had it painted. Peppi came and had a look. Tears came into his eyes. 'You are a bad boy,' he said. 'One day you will get into trouble. You think you are smart. One day you will be too smart.'

I just laughed and walked off. I knew he wouldn't do anything. He was too soft-hearted. He was always giving free ice-creams to kids that had no money. He felt sorry for poor people. The silly fool.

There were a lot of stories going round about that ice-cream. People said that it was good for you. Some kids said that it made you better when you were sick.

One of the teachers called it 'Happy Ice Cream.' I didn't believe it; it never made me happy.

All the same, there was something strange about it. Take Pimples Peterson for example. That wasn't his real name – I just called him that because he had a lot of pimples. Anyway, Peppi heard me calling Peterson 'Pimples'. 'You are a real mean boy,' he said. 'You are always picking on some one else, just because they are not like you.'

'Get lost, Peppi,' I said. 'Go and flog your ice-cream somewhere else.'

Peppi didn't answer me. Instead he spoke to Pimples. 'Here, eat this,' he told him. He handed Peterson an ice cream. It was the biggest ice cream I had ever seen. It was coloured purple. Peterson wasn't too sure about it. He didn't think he had enough money for such a big ice-cream.

'Go on,' said Mr Peppi. 'Eat it. I am giving it to you for nothing. It will get rid of your pimples.'

I laughed and laughed. Ice cream doesn't get rid of pimples, it *gives* you pimples. Anyway, the next day when Peterson came to school he had no pimples. Not one. I couldn't believe it. The ice-cream had cured his pimples.

There were some other strange things that happened too. There was a kid at the school who had a long nose. Boy, was it long. He looked like Pinocchio. When he blew it you could hear it a mile away. I called him 'Snozzle'. He didn't like being called Snozzle. He used to go red in the face when I said it, and that was every time that I saw him. He didn't say anything back – he was scared that I would punch him up.

Peppi felt sorry for Snozzle too. He gave him a small green ice cream every morning, for nothing. What a jerk. He never gave me a free ice cream.

You won't believe what happened but I swear it's true. Snozzle's nose began to grow smaller. Every day it grew a bit smaller. In the end it was just a normal nose. When it was the right size Peppi stopped giving him the green ice-creams.

I made up my mind to put a stop to this ice-cream business. Jerome Dadian had been eating ice-cream the day he got one hundred for Maths. It must have been the ice-cream making him smart. I wasn't going to have anyone doing as well as me. I was the smartest kid in the school, and that's the way I wanted it to stay. I wanted to get a look inside that ice-cream van to find out what was going on.

I knew where Peppi kept his van at night – he left it in a small lane behind his house. I waited until about eleven o'clock at night. Then I crept out of the house and down to Peppi's van. I took a crowbar, a bucket of sand, a torch and some bolt cutters with me.

There was no one around when I reached the van. I sprang the door open with the crow bar and shone my torch around inside. I had never seen so many tubs of ice-cream before. There was every flavour you could think of: there was apple and banana, cherry and mango, blackberry and watermelon and about fifty other flavours. Right at the end of the van were four bins with locks on them. I went over and had a look. It was just as I thought – these were his special flavours. Each one had writing on the top. This is what they said:

HAPPY ICE-CREAM for cheering people up.

NOSE ICE-CREAM for long noses.

PIMPLE ICE-CREAM for removing pimples.

SMART ICE-CREAM for smart alecs

Now I knew his secret. That rat Dadian had been eating Smart Ice- Cream; that's how he got one hundred for Maths. I knew there couldn't be anyone as clever as me. I decided to fix Peppi up once and for all. I took out the bolt cutters and cut the locks off the four bins; then I put sand into every bin in the van. Except for the Smart Ice-Cream. I didn't put any sand in that.

I laughed to myself. Peppi wouldn't sell much ice-cream now. Not unless he started a new flavour – Sand Ice-Cream. I looked at the Smart Ice-Cream. I decided to eat some; it couldn't do any harm. Not that I needed it – I was already about as smart as you could get. Anyway, I gave it a try. I ate the lot. Once I started I couldn't stop. It tasted good. It was delicious.

I left the van and went home to bed, but I couldn't sleep. To tell the truth, I didn't feel too good. So I decided to write this. Then if any funny business has been going on you people will know what happened. I think I have made a mistake. I don't think Dadian did get any Smart Ice Cream.

It iz the nekst day now. Somefing iz hapening to me. I don't feal quite az smart. I have bean trying to do a reel hard sum. It iz wun and wun. Wot duz wun and wun make? Iz it free or iz it for?

WUNDERPANTS

My Dad is not a bad sort of bloke. There are plenty who are much worse. But he does rave on a bit, like if you get muddy when you are catching frogs, or rip your pants when you are building a tree hut. Stuff like that.

Mostly we understand each other and I can handle him. What he doesn't know doesn't hurt him. If he knew that I kept Snot, my pet rabbit, under the bed, he wouldn't like it; so I don't tell him. That way he is happy, I am happy and Snot is happy.

There are only problems when he finds out what has been going on. Like the time that I wanted to see *Mad Max II*. The old man said it was a bad movie – too much blood and guts.

'It's too violent,' he said.

'But, Dad, that's not fair. All the other kids are going. I'll be the only one in the school who hasn't seen it.' I went on and on like this. I kept nagging. In the end he gave in – he wasn't a bad old boy. He usually let me have what I wanted after a while. It was easy to get around him.

The trouble started the next morning. He was cleaning his teeth in the bathroom, making noises, humming and gurgling – you know the sort of thing. Suddenly he stopped. Everything went quiet. Then he came into the kitchen. There was toothpaste all around his mouth; he looked like a mad tiger. He was frothing at the mouth.

'What's this?' he said. He was waving his toothbrush about. 'What's this on my toothbrush?' Little grey hairs were sticking out of it. 'How did these hairs get on my toothbrush? Did you have my toothbrush, David?'

He was starting to get mad. I didn't know whether to own up or not. Parents always tell you that if you own up they will let you off. They say that they won't do anything if you are honest – no punishment.

I decided to give it a try. 'Yes,' I said. 'I used it yesterday.'

He still had toothpaste on his mouth. He couldn't talk properly. 'What are these little grey hairs?' he asked.

'I used it to brush my pet mouse,' I answered.

'Your what?' he screamed.

'My mouse.'

He started jumping up and down and screaming. He ran around in circles holding his throat, then he ran into the bathroom and started washing his mouth out. There was a lot of splashing and gurgling. He was acting like a madman.

I didn't know what all the fuss was about. All that yelling just over a few mouse hairs.

After a while he came back into the kitchen. He kept opening and shutting his mouth as if he could taste something bad. He had a mean look in his eye – real mean.

94

'What are you thinking of?' he yelled at the top of his voice. 'Are you crazy or something? Are you trying to kill me? Don't you know that mice carry germs? They are filthy things. I'll probably die of some terrible disease.'

He went on and on like this for ages. Then he said, 'And don't think that you are going to see *Mad Max II*. You can sit at home and think how stupid it is to brush a mouse with someone else's toothbrush.'

2

I went back to my room to get dressed. Dad just didn't understand about that mouse. It was a special mouse, a very special mouse indeed. It was going to make me a lot of money: fifty dollars, in fact. Every year there was a mouse race in Smith's barn. The prize was fifty dollars. And my mouse, Swift Sam, had a good chance of winning. But I had to look after him. That's why I brushed him with a toothbrush.

I knew that Swift Sam could beat every other mouse except one. There was one mouse I wasn't sure about. It was called Mugger and it was owned by Scrag Murphy, the toughest kid in the town. I had never seen his mouse, but I knew it was fast. Scrag Murphy fed it on a special diet.

That is what I was thinking about as I dressed. I went over to the cupboard to get a pair of underpants. There were none there. 'Hey, Mum,' I yelled out. 'I am out of underpants.'

Mum came into the room holding something terrible. Horrible. It was a pair of home made underpants. 'I made these for you, David,' she said. 'I bought the material at the Op Shop. There was just the right amount of material for one pair of underpants.'

'I'm not wearing those,' I told her. 'No way. Never.'

'What's wrong with them?' said Mum. She sounded hurt.

'They're pink,' I said. 'And they've got little pictures of fairies on them. I couldn't wear them. Everyone would laugh. I would be the laughing stock of the school.'

Underpants with fairies on them and pink. I nearly freaked out. I thought about what Scrag Murphy would say if he ever heard about them. I went red just thinking about it.

Just then Dad poked his head into the room. He still had that mean look in his eye. He was remembering the toothbrush. 'What's going on now?' he asked in a black voice.

'Nothing,' I said. 'I was just thanking Mum for making me these nice underpants.' I pulled on the fairy pants and quickly covered them up with my jeans. At least no one else would know I had them on. That was one thing to be thankful for.

The underpants felt strange. They made me tingle all over. And my head felt light. There was something not quite right about those underpants – and I am not talking about the fairies.

3

I had breakfast and went out to the front gate. Pete was waiting for me. He is my best mate; we always walk to school together. 'Have you got your running shoes?' he asked.

'Oh no,' I groaned. 'I forgot. It's the cross country race today.' I went back and got my running shoes. I came back out walking very slowly. I was thinking about the race. I would have to go to the changing rooms and get changed in front of Scrag Murphy and all the other boys. They would all laugh their heads off when they saw my fairy underpants.

We walked through the park on the way to school. There was a big lake in the middle. 'Let's chuck some stones,' said Pete. 'See who can throw the furthest.' I didn't even answer. I was feeling weak in the stomach. 'What's the matter with you?' he asked. 'You look like death warmed up.'

I looked around. There was no one else in the park. 'Look at this,' I said. I undid my fly and showed Pete the underpants. His eyes bugged out like organ stops; then he started to laugh. He fell over on the grass and laughed his silly head off. Tears rolled down his cheeks. He really thought it was funny. Some friend.

After a while Pete stopped laughing. 'You poor thing,' he said. 'What are you going to do? Scrag Murphy and the others will never let you forget it.'

We started throwing stones into the lake. I didn't try very hard. My heart wasn't in it. 'Hey,' said Pete. 'That was a good shot. It went right over to the other side.' He was right. The stone had reached the other side of the lake. No one had ever done that before; it was too far.

I picked up another stone. This time I threw as hard as I could. The stone went right over the lake and disappeared over some trees. 'Wow,' yelled Pete. 'That's the best shot I've ever seen. No one can throw that far.' He looked at me in a funny way.

My skin was all tingling. 'I feel strong,' I said. 'I feel as if I can do anything.' I went over to a park bench. It was a large concrete one. I lifted it up with one hand. I held it high over my head. I couldn't believe it.

Pete just stood there with his mouth hanging open. He couldn't believe it either. I felt great. I jumped for joy. I sailed high into the air. I went up three metres. 'What a jump,' yelled Pete.

My skin was still tingling. Especially under the under-pants. 'It's the underpants,' I said. 'The underpants are giving me strength.' I grinned. 'They are not underpants. They are *wunderpants.*'

'Super Jocks,' said Pete. We both started cackling like a couple of hens. We laughed until our sides ached.

4

I told Pete not to tell anyone about the wunderpants. We decided to keep it a secret. Nothing much happened until the cross country race that afternoon. All the boys went to the changing room to put on their running gear. Scrag Murphy was there. I tried to get into my shorts without him seeing my wunderpants, but it was no good. He noticed them as soon as I dropped my jeans.

'Ah ha,' he shouted. 'Look at baby britches. Look at his fairy pants.' Everyone looked. They all started to laugh. How embarrassing. They were all looking at the fairies on my wunderpants.

Scrag Murphy was a big, fat bloke. He was really tough. He came over and pulled the elastic on my wunderpants. Then he let it go. 'Ouch,' I said. 'Cut that out. That hurts.'

'What's the matter, little Diddums?' he said. 'Can't

you take it?' He shoved me roughly against the wall. I wasn't going to let him get away with that, so I pushed him back – just a little push. He went flying across the room and crashed into the wall on the other side. I just didn't know my own strength. That little push had sent him all that way. It was the wunderpants.

Scrag Murphy looked at me with shock and surprise that soon turned to a look of hate. But he didn't say anything. No one said anything. They were all thinking I was going to get my block knocked off next time I saw Scrag Murphy.

About forty kids were running in the race. We had to run through the countryside, following markers that had been put out by the teachers. It was a hot day, so I decided to wear a pair of shorts but no top.

As soon as the starting gun went I was off like a flash. I had kept my wunderpants on and they were working really well. I went straight out to the front. I had never run so fast before. As I ran along the road I passed a man on a bike. He tried to keep up with me, but he couldn't. Then I passed a car. This was really something. This was great.

I looked behind. None of the others were in sight – I was miles ahead. The trail turned off the road and into the bush. I was running along a narrow track in the forest. After a while I came to a small creek. I was hot so I decided to have a dip. After all, the others were a long way behind; I had plenty of time. I took off my shorts and running shoes, but I left the wunderpants on. I wasn't going to part with them.

I dived into the cold water. It was refreshing. I lay on my back looking at the sky. Life was good. These wunderpants were terrific. I would never be scared of Scrag Murphy while I had them on.

Then something started to happen – something terrible. The wunderpants started to get tight. They hurt. They were shrinking. They were shrinking smaller and smaller. The pain was awful. I had to get them off. I struggled and wriggled; they were so tight they cut into my skin. In the end I got them off, and only just in time. They shrank so small that they would only just fit over my thumb. I had a narrow escape. I could have been killed by the shrinking wunderpants.

Just then I heard voices coming. It was the others in the race. I was trapped – I couldn't get out to put on my shorts. There were girls in the race. I had to stay in the middle of the creek in the nude.

5

It took quite a while for all the others to run by. They were all spread out along the track. Every time I went to get out of the pool, someone else would come. After a while Pete stopped at the pool. 'What are you doing?' he said. 'Even super jocks won't help you win from this far back.'

'Keep going,' I said. 'I'll tell you about it later.' I didn't want to tell him that I was in the nude. Some girls were with him.

Pete and the girls took off along the track. A bit later the last runner arrived. It was Scrag Murphy. He couldn't run fast – he was carrying too much weight. 'Well, look at this,' he said. 'It's little Fairy Pants. And what's this we have here?' He picked up my shorts and running shoes from the bank of the creek. Then he ran off with them.

'Come back,' I screamed. 'Bring those back here.' He didn't take any notice. He just laughed and kept running.

I didn't know what to do. I didn't have a stitch of clothing. I didn't even have any shoes. I was starting to feel cold; the water was freezing. I was covered in goose pimples and my teeth were chattering. In the end I had to get out. I would have frozen to death if I stayed in the water any longer.

I went and sat on a rock in the sun and tried to think of a way to get home without being seen. It was all right in the bush. I could always hide behind a tree if someone came. But once I reached the road I would be in trouble; I couldn't just walk along the road in the nude.

Then I had an idea. I looked at the tiny underpants. I couldn't put them on, but they still might work. I put them over my thumb and jumped. It was no good. It was just an ordinary small jump. I picked up a stone and threw it. It only went a short way, not much of a throw at all. The pants were too small, and I was my weak old self again.

I lay down on the rock in the sun. Ants started to crawl over me. Then the sun went behind a cloud. I started to get cold, but I couldn't walk home – not in the raw. I felt miserable. I looked around for something to wear, but there was nothing. Just trees, bushes and grass.

I knew I would have to wait until dark. The others would all have gone home by now. Pete would think I had gone home, and my parents would think I was at his place. No one was going to come and help me.

I started to think about Scrag Murphy. He was going to pay for this. I would get him back somehow.

Time went slowly, but at last it started to grow dark. I made my way back along the track. I was in bare feet and I kept standing on stones. Branches reached out and scratched me in all sorts of painful places. Then I started to think about snakes. What if I stood on one?

There were all sorts of noises in the dark. The moon had gone in, and it was hard to see where I was going. I have to admit it: I was scared. Scared stiff. To cheer myself up I started to think about what I was going to do to Scrag Murphy. Boy, was he going to get it.

At last I came to the road. I was glad to be out of the bush. My feet were cut and bleeding and I hobbled along. Every time a car went by I had to dive into the bushes. I couldn't let myself get caught in the headlights of the cars.

I wondered what I was going to do when I reached the town. There might be people around. I broke off a branch from a bush and held it in front of my 'you know what'. It was prickly, but it was better than nothing.

By the time I reached the town it was late. There was no one around. But I had to be careful – someone might come out of a house at any minute. I ran from tree to tree and wall to wall, hiding in the shadows as I went. Lucky for me the moon was in and it was very dark.

Then I saw something that gave me an idea – a phone box. I opened the door and stepped inside. A dim light shone on my naked body. I hoped that no one was look-ing. I had no money, but Pete had told me that if you yell into the ear-piece they can hear you on the other end. It was worth a try. I dialled our home number. Dad anwered. 'Yes,' he said.

'I'm in the nude,' I shouted. 'I've lost my clothes. Help. Help.'

'Hello, hello. Who's there?' said Dad.

I shouted at the top of my voice, but Dad just kept saying 'Hello'. He sounded cross. Then I heard him say to Mum, 'It's probably that boy up to his tricks again.' He hung up the phone.

I decided to make a run for it. It was the only way. I dropped my bush and started running. I went for my life. I reached our street without meeting a soul. I thought I was safe, but I was wrong. I crashed right into someone and sent them flying. It was old Mrs Jeeves from across the road.

'Sorry,' I said. 'Gee, I'm sorry.' I helped her stand up. She was a bit short sighted and it was dark. She hadn't noticed that I didn't have any clothes on. Then the moon came out – the blazing moon. I tried to cover my naked-ness with my hands, but it was no good.

'Disgusting,' she screeched. 'Disgusting. I'll tell your father about this.'

I ran home as fast as I could. I went in the back door and jumped into bed. I tried to pretend that I was asleep. Downstairs I could hear Mrs Jeeves yelling at Dad; then the front door closed. I heard his footsteps coming up the stairs.

6

Well, I really copped it. I was in big trouble. Dad went on and on. 'What are you thinking of, lad? Running around in the nude. Losing all your clothes. What will the neighbours think?' He went on like that for about a week. I couldn't tell him the truth – he wouldn't believe it. No one would. The only ones who knew the whole story were Pete and I.

Dad grounded me for a month. I wasn't allowed out of

the house except to go to school. No pictures, no swimming, nothing. And no pocket money either.

It was a bad month. Very bad indeed. At school Scrag Murphy gave me a hard time. He called me 'Fairy Pants'. Every one thought it was a great joke, and there was nothing I could do about it. He was just too big for me, and his mates were all tough guys.

'This is serious,' said Pete. 'We have to put Scrag Murphy back in his box. They are starting to call me 'Friend Of Fairy Pants' now. We have to get even.'

We thought and thought but we couldn't come up with anything. Then I remembered the mouse race in Smith's barn. 'We will win the mouse race,' I shouted. 'It's in a month's time. We can use the next month to train my mouse.'

'That's it,' said Pete. 'The prize is fifty dollars. Scrag Murphy thinks he is going to win. It will really get up his nose if we take off the prize.'

I went and fetched Swift Sam. 'He's small,' I said. 'But he's fast. I bet he can beat Murphy's mouse. It's called Mugger.'

We started to train Swift Sam. Every day after school we took him around a track in the back yard. We tied a piece of cheese on the end of a bit of string. Swift Sam chased after it as fast as he could. After six laps we gave him the piece of cheese to eat. At the start he could do six laps in ten minutes. By the end of the month he was down to three minutes.

'Scrag Murphy, look out,' said Pete with a grin. 'We are really going to beat the pants off you this time.'

7

The day of the big race came at last. There were about one hundred kids in Smith's barn. No adults knew about it – they would probably have stopped it if they knew. It cost fifty cents to get in. That's where the prize money came from. A kid called Tiger Gleeson took up the money and gave out the prize at the end. He was the organiser of the whole thing.

Scrag Murphy was there, of course. 'It's in the bag,' he swaggered. 'Mugger can't lose. I've fed him on a special diet. He is the fittest mouse in the county. He will eat Swift Sam, just you wait and see.'

I didn't say anything. But I was very keen to see his mouse, Mugger. Scrag Murphy had it in a box. No one had seen it yet.

'Right,' said Tiger. 'Get out your mice.' I put Swift Sam down on the track. He looked very small. He started sniffing around. I hoped he would run as fast with the other mice there – he hadn't had any match practice before. Then the others put their mice on the track. Everyone except Scrag Murphy. He still had Mugger in the box.

Scrag Murphy put his hand in the box and took out Mugger. He was the biggest mouse I had ever seen. He was at least ten times as big as Swift Sam. 'Hey,' said Pete. 'That's not a mouse. That's a rat. You can't race a rat. It's not fair.'

'It's not a rat,' said Scrag Murphy in a threatening voice. 'It's just a big mouse. I've been feeding it up'. I looked at it again. It was a rat all right. It was starting to attack the mice.

'We will take a vote,' said Tiger. 'All those that

think it is a rat, put your hands up.' He counted all the hands.

'Fifty,' he said. 'Now all those who say that Mugger is a mouse put your hands up.' He counted again.

'Fifty two. Mugger is a mouse.'

Scrag Murphy and his gang started to cheer. He had brought all his mates with him. It was a put-up job.

'Right,' said Tiger Gleeson. 'Get ready to race.'

8

There were about ten mice in the race – or I should say nine mice and one rat. Two rats if you counted Scrag Murphy. All the owners took out their string and cheese. 'Go,' shouted Tiger Gleeson.

Mugger jumped straight on to a little mouse next to him and bit it on the neck. The poor thing fell over and lay still. 'Boo,' yelled some of the crowd.

Swift Sam ran to the front straight away. He was going really well. Then Mugger started to catch up. It was neck and neck for five laps. First Mugger would get in front, then Swift Sam. Everyone in the barn went crazy. They were yelling their heads off.

By the sixth lap Mugger started to fall behind. All the other mice were not in the race. They had been lapped twice by Mugger and Swift Sam. But Mugger couldn't keep up with Swift Sam; he was about a tail behind. Suddenly something terrible happened. Mugger jumped onto Swift Sam's tail and grabbed it in his teeth. The crowd started to boo. Even Scrag Murphy's mates were booing.

But Swift Sam kept going. He didn't stop for a second. He just pulled that great rat along after him. It rolled over and over behind the little mouse. Mugger held on for grim death, but he couldn't stop Swift Sam. 'What a mouse,' screamed the crowd as Swift Sam crossed the finish line still towing Mugger behind him.

Scrag Murphy stormed off out of the barn. He didn't even take Mugger with him. Tiger handed me the fifty dollars. Then he held up Swift Sam. 'Swift Sam is the winner,' he said. 'The only mouse in the world with its own little pair of fairy underpants.'